O9-ABF-833

From bump to baby and beyond…

Whether she's expecting or they're adopting—
a special arrival is on its way!

Follow the tears and triumphs
as these couples find their lives
blessed with the magic of parenthood….

And look out for a special New Year delivery
from Raye Morgan in

The Italian's Forgotten Baby

January 2010

Dear Reader,

The prewriting phase of a book is always interesting for me. Usually I come up with my characters first, figure out what their issues and conflicts are, and then I build a plot around them. Sometimes doing so is easy. Sometimes it's not. The plot for this book fell into the latter category.

Indeed, Logan and Mallory's story went through so many incarnations before I ever began writing the first chapter that I finally gave up numbering my outlines. What eventually became the synopsis for *Confidential: Expecting!* actually bore the moniker "Logan and Mallory Newest Version."

Thankfully, writing Logan and Mallory's story proved to be much easier than writing that synopsis.

I hope you enjoy *Confidential: Expecting!* As always, I'd love to hear what you think. You can reach me through my Web site at www.jackiebraun.com.

Best wishes,

Jackie Braun

JACKIE BRAUN
Confidential: Expecting!

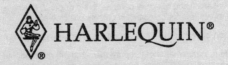

TORONTO • NEW YORK • LONDON
AMSTERDAM • PARIS • SYDNEY • HAMBURG
STOCKHOLM • ATHENS • TOKYO • MILAN • MADRID
PRAGUE • WARSAW • BUDAPEST • AUCKLAND

If you purchased this book without a cover you should be aware
that this book is stolen property. It was reported as "unsold and
destroyed" to the publisher, and neither the author nor the
publisher has received any payment for this "stripped book."

Recycling programs
for this product may
not exist in your area.

ISBN-13: 978-0-373-17630-4

CONFIDENTIAL: EXPECTING!

First North American Publication 2009.

Copyright © 2009 by Jackie Braun Fridline.

All rights reserved. Except for use in any review, the reproduction or
utilization of this work in whole or in part in any form by any electronic,
mechanical or other means, now known or hereafter invented, including
xerography, photocopying and recording, or in any information storage
or retrieval system, is forbidden without the written permission of the
publisher, Harlequin Enterprises Limited, 225 Duncan Mill Road,
Don Mills, Ontario, Canada M3B 3K9.

This is a work of fiction. Names, characters, places and incidents are
either the product of the author's imagination or are used fictitiously,
and any resemblance to actual persons, living or dead, business
establishments, events or locales is entirely coincidental.

This edition published by arrangement with Harlequin Books S.A.

® and TM are trademarks of the publisher. Trademarks indicated with
® are registered in the United States Patent and Trademark Office, the
Canadian Trade Marks Office and in other countries.

www.eHarlequin.com

Printed in U.S.A.

Jackie Braun is a three-time RITA® Award finalist, three-time National Readers' Choice Award finalist and a past winner of the Rising Star Award. She lives in Michigan, with her husband and two sons, and can be reached through her Web site at www.jackiebraun.com.

"Unlike my heroine, I'd never be able to keep the news of a baby confidential. I think half the free world knew my husband and I were adopting a second child before the agency received our application."

—Jackie Braun

For Don and Jean Fridline,
who lived a love story. I miss you both.

CHAPTER ONE

"Is THIS seat taken?"

Mallory Stevens knew that deep, seductive voice. As best she could, she braced herself before looking up into a pair of smiling gray-green eyes and a face that would have made Adonis seem homely by comparison. It was no use.

Zip, zap, zing!

Just that fast, her hormones snapped to attention and her limbs turned liquid. It was a bizarre reaction, though she'd be lying if she labeled it unpleasant. Nor was it unprecedented. She'd experienced its twin a week earlier when she'd met Logan Bartholomew for the first time.

They'd been in his office, and she'd written it off then as a fluke. She'd been working too many hours. She'd barely slept the night before. She'd gone without the company of a man for *way, way* too long.

But a fluke didn't happen twice. When it did, and it involved a member of the opposite sex, it was called something else: attraction.

Mallory sucked in a breath before letting it out slowly between her teeth. She certainly had nothing against mingling with members of the opposite sex. She liked men, but she had a rule about mixing business with pleasure. It was a no-no. Logan Batholomew was business, even if everything about him made her body hum with pleasure.

"You're welcome to join me, Doctor," she told him. Though it took an effort, her tone was blessedly nonchalant. She hoped the smile she sent him was the same.

He folded his athletic frame into the chair, managing to look both elegant and masculine. For the umpteenth time in their short acquaintance, she found herself thinking his gorgeous looks were wasted on the radio. He hosted a call-in program that had all of Chicago talking.

"I thought we'd agreed it was just Logan," he said.

Mallory knew he was wrong. Even though, now that *he* was here, sitting through the Windy City Women of Action luncheon she'd been assigned to cover held far more appeal, a qualifier such as *just* didn't apply when it came to Logan. Everything about the guy was off the charts, from his leading-man looks and tri-athlete physique to the way his show had burned its way to the top of the ratings in a little over a year. It was no wonder he'd been voted Chicago's most eligible bachelor in a recent poll sponsored by her newspaper.

As a reporter, Mallory reminded herself that she was interested in more than his heart-palpitating appeal and sigh-worthy exterior. She was interested in a story and she smelled one here. Not necessarily the sort that went with his sophisticated cologne and designer tie, and certainly not the trivial one that had landed her in his office the week before.

In her experience, no one was ever as perfect as this guy appeared to be with his Harvard degree and penchant for supporting worthwhile causes. She intended to unearth the skeletons in his closet and then expose each and every one of them. Maybe then her editor would forgive her for the embarrassing faux pas that had the newspaper's lawyers fending off a libel suit and Mallory writing the kind of general assignment fluff that usually went to the college interns.

"I should thank you for the article you did on my commencement address to the students and faculty at Chesterfield Alternative High School," he said.

Fluff, definitely. So much so that the airy advance had wound up buried in the bowels of the *Chicago Herald*'s Lifestyles section.

"You read it?" she asked, equally surprised that he'd found it.

"All four paragraphs," came his dry reply.

Truth be told, Mallory had had to pad it with his background to make it that long. God, she missed her city hall beat. Two months of writing nonsense had her feeling like a carnivore at a vegetarians' convention. She needed meat, the rarer the better, and unless her instincts were wrong, Logan was prime rib.

Angling her head to one side, she said, "So, any truth to the rumor I heard that *Doctor in the Know* might go national? Or that a certain cable television network has made you an offer for a prime-time program?"

If he was surprised by her questions, it didn't show. He didn't so much as blink. Rather, in a bland voice, he inquired, "On the record or off?"

"On, of course," she replied.

"Well then, no."

She lifted one brow. "And off the record?"

Logan leaned toward her, close enough that she could feel the heat radiating from his skin. She pictured his mouth, lips barely an inch from making contact with her earlobe when he whispered, "No comment."

In spite of herself, Mallory shivered. The man was downright lethal, a straight shot of sex outfitted in a suit that probably cost the equivalent of a month's worth of her take-home pay. She'd splurged on the black pencil skirt and tan fitted jacket she was wearing, but they were hardly designer label. Clearly, she was in the wrong profession, not that she had any plans to change. She loved her job. Until lately, it had been by far the most satisfying and reliable thing in her life. She intended it to be that way again.

Leaning back in her chair, Mallory smiled at Logan. "I'll find out eventually, you know. Ferreting out people's secrets is what I do best."

"I'd heard that about you," he replied amiably. "In fact, my agent called to warn me to be on my toes before you came to my office for the interview last week. She said you were a regular pit bull."

"A pit bull, hmm?" Mallory ran her tongue over her teeth.

"Actually, she called you a *rabid* pit bull." Logan chuckled as if to soften the description and added, "I hope I haven't offended you."

"Offended me?" She exhaled sharply. "Please. I'm flattered by her description."

"I don't think she meant it as a compliment."

"I'm sure she didn't." Still Mallory shrugged. "I'll take it as one, anyway. In my line of work I believe in going for the throat. It's what yields the best results."

Her gaze lowered as she said this. Loosen that silk tie and undo the top button at his collar and Logan Bartholomew had one very delicious-looking neck.

"What about outside of work?"

His question startled her from her musings. Mallory's gaze shot back to his face, where a potent and very male smile greeted her.

"Wh-what do you mean?" She hated that she'd actually stammered like a shy schoolgirl conversing with the football team's star quarterback.

"What do you do after hours? You know, to unwind?" His expression was just this side of challenging.

"I tend to work late." Then she went home alone, picking up some takeout on the way to her walk-up half a block from an El stop. Once she'd changed out of her work attire, she usually ate while watching the television before crashing for the night on the queen-size bed in her room. Alone.

"No…boyfriend?" he inquired.

Her eyes narrowed. "Not at the moment." Though not for two years was closer to reality.

"Hmm."

"Are you analyzing me, Doctor?" Mallory asked.

"Logan," he reminded her with an affable grin.

"Yes, but at the moment you're sounding an awful lot like someone with a degree in psychiatry."

"Ah." He grimaced, seemingly for effect. "Sorry about that. A hazard of my profession, I'm afraid. I just find it hard to believe that someone as bright, interesting and, well, attractive as you are isn't in a serious relationship."

"Good save." She said it dryly in the hope of camouflaging the spurt of pleasure she'd experienced upon hearing his compliments.

Bright, interesting, attractive. What woman wouldn't want to be considered all three, especially by a man who looked like this one?

The servers came around then with their salads and baskets of bread. Mallory selected a hard roll. At their first meeting, Logan's time had been limited, so she'd only had the opportunity to ask him questions related to the commencement address. Now, under the guise of small talk, she asked him, "What about you? What do you do when you're not at the radio station?"

"Well, for starters, I like to eat." He forked up some mixed baby greens that were coated in raspberry vinaigrette.

"Yes, you look it." Logan was a walking advertisement for physical fitness. If the man looked this good with his clothes on, she could only imagine how he appeared sans his professional attire. The thought had her coughing.

He swatted her back. "Are you all right?"

"Fine," she managed. "Never better. You were saying something about eating?"

"I like food. For that reason, I learned how to cook."

Mallory squinted at him. "Learned how to cook as in learned how to work the microwave oven or learned how to cook as in—"

"I know my way around the kitchen," he inserted. "For instance, tonight I'm planning to grill a marinated flank steak and then pair it with rice noodles and a simple green salad."

Her mouth watered. "Just for you?"

"Most likely."

"I'm impressed." And she was. "I've never gotten much beyond boiling water, which is actually pretty handy considering it's one of the most important steps in making macaroni and cheese."

"From a box," he acknowledged. "There are other ways, you know."

No, she didn't know. In her albeit limited experience, all that was necessary was to bring the water to a boil and add the elbow noodles. When they were cooked, she drained the water, drizzled in a quarter cup of milk and stirred in the packet of a dry, cheeselike substance. *Voilà.* Dinner.

Logan was saying, "I've found cooking to be a surprising release for my creative energy."

She found his admission surprising, as well, but as secrets went, well, news that Chicago's new favorite son liked to play chef in his off hours wasn't likely to score Mallory many points with her editor.

So, she asked, "What else do you do in your spare time? I know you don't frequent the hot night spots."

She'd checked.

"I'm a little old for that."

"Thirty-six isn't exactly ancient." Especially when it came packaged in broad shoulders, narrow hips and topped off with a full head of gorgeous sandy hair.

The shoulders in question rose. "Night clubs aren't really my thing."

They weren't Mallory's, either. Sure, she liked to dance, sip a cocktail and have a good time every now and then, but she'd long ago grown out of the meat-market scene so many of the city's hottest spots promoted. These days when she went out it was usually with a former college roommate for margaritas at a little Mexican restaurant that was one step above dive status.

"So, what is your thing?" she asked.

Logan said nothing for a long moment. Rather, he studied her with a gaze that was both challenging and assessing. Which is why Mallory found herself holding her breath until he finally replied, "I like to sail."

The air whooshed from her lungs. "Sail. As in boats?" Mallory couldn't help feeling disappointed. Unless he was going to tell her he kept narcotics in the hold this revelation was as newsworthy as the tidbit about playing chef.

"Is there any other kind?" He was smiling. "My parents had a catamaran when I was a boy. I loved being out on it. So, I bought a thirty-one-footer a few years back. I take her out on Lake Michigan as often as I can. Even so, the season's just too damn short here."

Mallory didn't consider herself to be the romantic sort, yet she had no problem picturing Logan standing on a teak deck, manning the helm of a sailboat as the Chicago skyline grew small at his back and the deep aquamarine waters of the great lake beckoned.

"Sounds nice," she said in a voice just this side of wispy. Good Lord, what was wrong with her?

"It is. Especially first thing in morning. There's nothing like sitting on deck, drinking a cup of coffee and watching the sun crest the horizon."

Mallory swallowed. Focus, she coached herself, when her mind threatened to meander a second time. "You make it sound like you sleep on your boat."

"I've been known to. It's peaceful out there, you know? None of the city noise. Only lapping water and the occasional cry of gulls."

She thought about the El train that rumbled past her apartment at regular intervals. As far as she was concerned, what he spoke of was heaven. That was before she pictured him clad in…hmm…what did the good doctor wear to bed? That question brought another one to mind.

"Do you sleep there alone?" When his brows rose, she amended her query. "Who do you go sailing with?"

Logan's laughter rumbled, deep and rich, dancing up

her spine like a flat stone skipping over water. "Are you asking if I'm involved with someone?"

She cleared her throat, kept her tone reporter-neutral. "A lot of single women who read the *Herald* are dying to know just how eligible of a bachelor you are."

"It's that damned poll."

"Yes," she said dryly. "Every man in Chicago wishes he were so lucky as to find his name on it."

"Do I have you to thank for my…providence?" he inquired.

Mallory shook her head. "I wasn't part of the Lifestyles team then."

He was undeterred. "But are you one of them? You know, the voters, those women interested in my personal life?"

"Not a voter, no. But you bet I am interested in your personal life." She pulled a pen and slim notepad from the purse hanging over the back of her chair. "So?"

Some of the good humor leaked out of Logan's expression when he said, "I didn't realize that you were sent to this luncheon to cover me."

Was that censure she spied in his gaze or disappointment? Mallory didn't like seeing either one, but neither was she willing to back down. "Rabid pit bull," Logan's agent had called her. Well, she'd earned the reputation for a reason.

"Sorry. Hazard of my profession. And I can't help thinking you make a far more interesting story than the winner of this year's Action Award." She tilted her head in the direction of the head table. "You're a local celebrity, Logan. Homegrown, self-made and very success-ful. You're also a bit mysterious. Other than where you earned your degree and some of your vital statistics, not much is known about you."

He folded his arms over his chest. "I like my privacy."

"Yes, and readers like to invade it." Mallory angled her head to one side. "It's good public relations to toss them a bone every now and then. You know, since they're the ones who tune in to your radio program and all." Going for the jugular, she added, "In a very real sense, you could say you owe your success to them."

"Well, when you put it that way." A smile spread slowly across his face. Lethal, Mallory thought again, as her hormones popped around inside her like the numbered balls in a bingo machine. She found herself actually leaning toward him, drawn the way a moth is to a flame. And so it came as little surprise when heat began to spiral through her.

"Well?" Was that her voice that sounded so breath-less, so damned eager?

"I'm not…in a relationship."

She moistened her lips, leaned back. "Ah."

What exactly did that mean? Men, she knew first-hand, defined relationships differently than women did.

"Any other questions?" Logan asked.

Mallory had dozens of them, and the man, her prime-rib ticket to workplace redemption, was offering her the opportunity to ask them. Unfortunately, with him looking at her in that assessing way, her mind had gone blank. She shook her head slowly, thankful when their entrees arrived and saved her from appearing tongue-tied, which, for the first time in her professional life, she was.

They ate their rubber chicken and overcooked rice pilaf in virtual silence; all the while Mallory recalled his mention of grilled marinated flank steak. It was almost a relief when the servers cleared away their plates and the award program began. Except that, as the president of the women's club blathered on about the recipient's many virtues, from the corner of her eye, Mallory spied Logan watching her.

What on earth was he thinking?

Logan studied Mallory. He'd meant it when he'd told her she was bright, interesting and attractive.

Attractive. Hell, she was downright lovely with all that rich brown hair framing an oval face that was dominated by the most amazing pair of big dark eyes he'd ever seen. Despite her physical beauty, it was her personality that captivated him. He liked smart women. The smarter the better. Add in pretty and, well, it was a lethal combination as far as he was concerned. Mallory certainly hit the mark. That in itself was a problem.

Logan had met her kind once before, years ago. He'd fallen hard at the time, so hard he'd almost made it to the altar, ready and willing to promise his undying love and devotion. A month before their nuptials, however, his fiancée had called off the wedding. Felicia had claimed to need time and space. She'd needed to think, to reflect. What became clear was she hadn't needed him. She married someone else.

It had been nearly a decade since then. Logan had heard from her only once, just after her wedding. She'd sent him a letter, the postmark read Portland, Oregon. In the brief note, she'd asked him to forgive her, but even if he'd wanted to, he couldn't. She'd included no forwarding address or phone number. He'd taken the hint. He'd been wary of commitment ever since.

That didn't mean he didn't like women or spending time with them. It just meant he didn't let things progress into anything serious.

He glanced over at Mallory. She was scribbling down notes, seemingly absorbed in the award recipient's less-than-exciting speech. As he watched her, his interest, among other things, was definitely piqued.

Rabid pit bull.

Logan's agent had been adamant that he should steer clear of this particular reporter. Mallory had a reputation for ruining people, Nina Lowman insisted. Maybe it was the masochist in him that considered her reputation a challenge. Besides, he could handle himself around reporters. He'd been doing it enough since his radio call-in program had staked out the top spot in the ratings.

So, as the luncheon wrapped up, Logan leaned over to Mallory and asked, "Since turnabout is fair play, I have a question for you."

"Oh?"

"What are you doing later this afternoon?"

She blinked, before her eyes narrowed. Why was it he found her suspicion sexy?

"Filing a story. Why?"

"How long will that take?"

"For this?" Her lips twisted, showing her distaste. It wasn't the first time he wondered why a reporter with her reputation had been sent to cover a minor story. "I need a couple of quotes from the winner, a quote from someone on the award committee and to tap out a couple of paragraphs summing up why the winner was selected."

"In other words, you could write it in your sleep," he concluded.

She rewarded his blunt assessment with a smile. "Once I do a couple of brief interviews it should take me half an hour, tops. Why?"

Logan was playing with fire, which wasn't like him. While he liked challenges, he wasn't one to take unnecessary risks. Still, he heard himself ask, "Have you ever seen the city from the water?"

"No," she said slowly.

"Well, if you want to, I dock my sailboat, the *Tangled Sheets*, at the yacht club. I'm planning to take her out around five."

Something flashed in her dark eyes. Interest? Excitement? Briefly he wondered whether it was the reporter or the woman responsible for whatever emotion it was. To his surprise, he found he didn't care.

"Which yacht club?" she asked.

Logan wasn't willing to make it too easy for her. So

he stood and, giving her a salute, walked backward a few steps toward the exit.

Just before turning he called, "You're a reporter, Mallory. If you really want to meet me, you'll figure it out."

CHAPTER TWO

DESPITE changing into a lightweight blouse and a pair of cropped trousers, Mallory was wilting in the late-afternoon heat by the time she arrived at Logan's slip at the Chicago Yacht Club. It didn't help that she'd nearly jogged the half-dozen blocks from the El stop. She had a car, but she often found public transportation less of a hassle than trying to find a place to park.

After leaving the luncheon, she'd hurried through her story, filing it after only a cursory second read and a run of her computer's spellchecker. It wasn't like her to rush, especially for a man. But then Logan was far more than that to her. He was a story.

Her *story* took her breath away when she caught sight of him standing with his feet planted shoulder-width apart on the deck of a sailboat. Behind him sunlight reflected off the smooth, aquamarine surface of the lake, making him look like something straight out of a fantasy.

His back was to her, a cell phone tucked between his ear and shoulder, so she took her time studying him.

He'd changed his clothing, too. Instead of the pricy suit he'd worn earlier, he was attired in a short-sleeved shirt that showed off a pair of muscled arms and casual tan slacks that fit nicely across a very fine and firm-looking butt. Mallory fanned herself. Damned heat. Though it was only June, the mercury had to be pushing one hundred degrees Fahrenheit in the shade.

On the barest wisp of a breeze, Logan's side of the conversation floated to her.

"You don't need to worry… No. Really. Do you know the saying 'Keep your friends close and your enemies closer'?" His laughter rumbled deep and rich before he continued. "Exactly… Yeah, I'll call you."

He said goodbye and flipped his phone closed. As soon as he turned and spotted Mallory, male interest lit up his eyes and a flush of embarrassment stained his cheeks.

He coughed. "I didn't realize you were here."

"Obviously."

His flush deepened.

Mallory could have pretended not to have overheard anything. That would have been the polite thing to do. But she was a reporter, which meant curiosity trumped politeness.

"So, which one am I?" When he frowned, she added helpfully, "Friend or enemy?"

She gave him credit. Logan pulled out of his flaming, death spiral with amazing speed and agility. But then, he was a veteran of talk radio and live broadcasts, which meant he was good at thinking on his feet.

Walking to the rail, he asked, "Which one do you consider yourself?"

"Ah. Very clever, turning the question around. Is that what they teach you to do in psychiatry school?"

"Among other things," he allowed.

Whatever remained of his embarrassment had evaporated completely by the time his hand clasped Mallory's to help her aboard. His palm was warm against hers, pleasantly so despite the heat. It seemed a shame when he removed it, though she supposed it would have been awkward if he had continued the contact.

"So," she said, filling in the silence.

"So." One side of his mouth lifted, but he backed up a step, and she liked knowing that she could keep him as off balance as he made her. Tucking his hands into the front pockets of his trousers, he said, "I wasn't sure you were coming or that you'd be able to find me."

Though the city had more than one yacht club, it hadn't taken much effort. His boat was registered. Besides, the Chicago Yacht Club, which dated to the late eighteen hundreds, was exclusive. It seemed the most likely spot for an up-and-coming celebrity who cherished his privacy.

Mallory nodded toward the bottle of red wine that was open and breathing on a small table topside. "I'd say you knew that I would."

He shrugged. "I was hopeful. Besides, I was banking on your journalistic instincts."

"I bank on them, too, since they rarely fail me."

"Should I be nervous?"

"You tell me," she replied.

"I guess that depends on why you're here."

"I was invited," she reminded him.

"So you were."

In truth, Mallory was still perplexed by Logan's spontaneous offer of an afternoon sail. It was one of the reasons she'd come. What exactly did the man have in mind?

"Why?" The question rent the silence with all the delicacy of a gull's cry.

"Excuse me?"

"Why did you invite me?"

"Well, that's blunt." He chuckled.

Mallory shrugged. "I don't believe in beating around the bush."

"No, I don't suppose you would." With an index finger, he tapped his cell phone. "You know, my agent wanted to know the answer to that very question, too."

"What did you tell her, besides not to worry?"

His brows furrowed. "Actually, I didn't have an answer for her."

"Besides the friends-and-enemies adage," Mallory remarked.

"Besides that," he agreed. "So, why did you come? And, yes, I'm turning the question around."

"Curiosity," she replied honestly. "How could I decline when I find you so intriguing?"

"I'm flattered, I think. Especially if that's the woman speaking rather than the reporter."

"They're one and the same, remember?"

Logan's gaze intensified. "Are you sure about that?"

She was, or at least she had been until he'd pinned her with that stare and baldly asked. The boat moved under her feet, a slight rolling motion that reminded her of the water bed she'd had as a teenager. She'd slept like a baby back then. These days she was lucky to snatch a few hours of uninterrupted slumber before her eyes snapped open and her mind began clicking away like a slide projector, flashing the items on her current to-do list at work along with the goals related to her long-range career plans.

"I'd love a glass of that wine," she said, opting to change the subject.

"I wouldn't mind some myself." As he poured it, he said, "How exactly did you find me? I only ask so I can prevent others from doing the same."

"Sorry." She shook her head and, after a sip of the Merlot, added, "As much as I'd like to help you out—not to mention, keep other reporters away—I can't reveal my sources."

He nodded sagely. "Bad form?"

"Right up there with a magician giving away the secret to how he saws his assistant in half," she said with sham seriousness.

His smile turned boyish and was all the more charming for it. "I've always wanted to know how that's done."

"I do," she couldn't help bragging. "Just after college I was assigned to do a feature on a guy who did a magic act at a local nightclub. After the interview, he showed me."

"But you won't tell me, will you?" Logan guessed.

"And ruin the illusion?"

"Right." Logan chuckled. "So, are you hungry?"

"I'm getting there," she replied casually.

In fact, Mallory was famished. She'd barely picked at her lunch, and breakfast—a toasted bagel with cream cheese eaten at her desk just after dawn—was a distant memory now.

"Good. I went ahead and made dinner."

Her mouth actually watered. "The marinated flank steak you mentioned at the luncheon?" When he nodded, she said, "Do you mean you actually cooked it here?"

"I cooked the meat topside on that portable gas grill, and the rest was prepared below deck."

The meal he'd described earlier seemed the sort one would make in a gourmet kitchen, so her tone was dubious when she asked, "You have an actual stove down there?"

He smiled. "Quarters may be a bit tight, but you'll find my boat has all the amenities of home."

Why did that simple sentence send heat curling through her veins?

"A-all?" she stammered, then cleared her throat. In a more professional tone, she inquired, "How is that possible? I mean, this thing is just—what?—thirty feet long."

"Thirty-one, actually. But you'd be surprised what can be fitted into that amount of space using a bit of ingenuity. Want a tour?"

"I'd love one," she said, even though the idea of moving below deck with him suddenly made her nervous. It wasn't Logan who made her wary. Her concern had more to do with herself. Story, she reminded herself for what seemed like the millionth time since meeting him.

Luckily she was given a reprieve. "Can you wait until after dinner?"

"Sure." She shrugged. "I'm in no hurry."

Mallory sat at the table and let Logan serve her since he seemed to have everything under control. More than under control, she decided, when he reappeared from below deck a few minutes later carrying two plates of artfully arranged food. The meal looked like something that would be right at home on the cover of *Bon Appetit*.

"Wow. If this tastes as good as it looks, I'll be in heaven."

She meant it. Even though unmasking Logan's qualifications in the kitchen would never earn her a Pulitzer, much less her editor's forgiveness, it was hard not to admire a man who could whip up a five-star meal aboard a boat in the late afternoon heat and barely break a sweat as evidenced by his dry brow.

Logan settled onto the chair opposite hers. "Thanks."

"Mmm. Heaven, definitely," Mallory remarked after her first bite of the marinated meat. It melted in her mouth like butter. Afterward, she raised her glass. "I have to toast the chef. I'm impressed."

"That's quite a compliment coming from you. I get

the feeling you're not the type of woman who is quick with the accolades."

"Only when they're earned."

He smiled and sipped his wine. After setting it aside, he said, "Then, I can't wait until you taste the cinnamon apple torte I made for dessert."

"That good?"

"Better," he assured her with a wink that scored a direct hit on her libido. "Forget accolades. You just might be rendered speechless."

"That would be a first." She laughed. "But then, you've already proved you're a man of many talents."

"Yes, and I'm looking forward to introducing you to another one of them later."

Heat began to build again. "Oh?"

"The sail." But Logan's crooked smile told Mallory he knew exactly which direction her thoughts had taken and that he enjoyed knowing he could inspire such a detour.

As their meal progressed, the conversation veered—or was it steered?—to her personal life. Mallory didn't like to talk about herself, but as a reporter she'd found that divulging a few details about her past often helped her sources loosen up. So, when he asked if she was a Chicago native, she told him, "No. Actually, I'm not a Midwestern girl at all. I grew up in a small town in Massachusetts."

"That explains the flattened vowels." He smiled. "What brought you to Chicago?"

Nothing too personal here. So she said, "College. I attended Northwestern on a scholarship."

"And then you were hired in at the *Herald*," he assumed.

"Eventually. I spent the first three months after I graduated working gratis as an intern in the hope the editors would notice my work and offer me a full-time job. At the time, even though the *Herald* had no posted openings in its newsroom, competition in general was fierce."

"You wanted to be sure you had a foot in the door. That was very industrious, if a bit risky." Still, he nodded in appreciation. "What did your parents think of your decision to work for free?"

She sipped her wine. "It's just my mom and she thought I'd lost my mind."

"Why would she think that?"

Laughter scratched her throat. "I didn't mean that literally, Doctor."

"Good, because I'm not on the clock. Well?"

More than being direct, his gaze made her feel…safe. That brought heat of a different sort. She felt as if she could tell him anything and he wouldn't judge her the way her mother always had. And still did.

"My mother thought I was being a fool. She wanted me to be financially independent and she didn't see how working for free was going to get me anywhere."

"Reasonable goal," he allowed.

"Yeah, except it was a mantra she beat me over the head with after my folks divorced."

"I...I guess I thought your father was no longer around. When I asked what your folks thought, you said it was just your mom."

"It is and has been." She had to work to keep the bitterness out of her tone. "My dad's not dead. He's a deadbeat."

"Ohh." He grimaced. "Sorry. How old were you?"

"Eleven. My mother had been a stay-at-home mom with no marketable job skills when their marriage ended. She had a hard time finding work. She didn't want me to wind up depending on a man."

Mallory reached for her wine, if for no other reason than that taking a sip would shut her up. The only other person she'd ever mentioned this to was Vicki, her college roommate, and then only after a few too many margaritas.

Because she had a good idea what Logan must be thinking, she decided to say it first. "That's not the reason I'm married to my job, though. I happen to really enjoy what I do."

"I don't doubt it." He sipped his wine, too.

It was time to shift the conversation's focus. "What about your family? Siblings?"

"One of each, both younger than me."

"And your parents? Are they still together?" She knew that they were, but saying so would make it seem like she'd done a background check on him. Which she had.

"Yep." Nostalgia warmed his smile. "They're going on forty years and they still hold hands."

The answer prompted a question she was only too happy to ask, since it would turn the spotlight away from her life. "And yet you're thirty-six and single. Why is that?"

A shadow fell across his face, there and gone so quickly she almost wondered if she'd imagined it. But then he offered a disarming smile—a defense mechanism?—that made her all the more curious.

"I guess you could say after the apple fell, it rolled far away from the tree."

This apple had, too, Mallory thought, stuffing memories of her childhood back into their cubbyhole. And for good reason in her case. But why would someone whose parents had what sounded like the perfect union be gun-shy when it came to commitment? It bore looking into. Later.

Now, she said, "Do your siblings still live in Chicago?"

She knew his parents did. The elder Bartholomews were no strangers to the newspaper's society pages.

"Yes. My sister, Laurel, attends Loyola. She's pushing thirty, has been taking classes for more than a decade and has yet to settle on a major. It drives my parents crazy. Luke, my brother, owns a restaurant."

"Locally?"

He nodded. "The Berkley Grill just a few blocks up from Navy Pier."

"I love that place!" Mallory exclaimed. "Especially the grilled portabella mushroom sandwich topped with provolone cheese."

"That's one of my favorites, too."

"Is your brother a chef, then?" she asked.

"No. Like me he can hold his own in the kitchen, but he's a businessman by trade, and he has a good eye for spotting potential." His voice was tinged with pride. "The restaurant needed a fresh menu, updated dining room and better marketing to capitalize on tourist traffic. Since he bought it and made the upgrades, the place has done pretty well, even in this economy, and earned free publicity with a spot in a Food Network special."

"Do you ever plug his place on your radio program?"

"That would be a conflict of interest and not terribly ethical. Besides, he doesn't need my help."

Mallory nodded.

His gaze narrowed. "Are you disappointed with my answer?"

"Of course not. Why would I be?"

He didn't reply directly. Instead, he lobbed a question of his own. "What made you decide to become a journalist?"

"Curiosity," she said again. "I like knowing why things happen the way they do. Why people make the choices they make. I'm rarely happy unless I'm getting to the bottom of things."

"Then what were you doing covering today's luncheon? Not much dirt to uncover there."

"Penance," Mallory muttered before she could think better of it.

She expected him to pounce on that, since getting to the bottom of things was one of the hallmarks of his profession, too. But just as he'd knocked her off balance with the offer of a sail, he surprised her now by changing the subject.

Rising from his seat he asked, "Are you ready for coffee and dessert?"

"Maybe just coffee." She stood, as well, and helped him collect the dishes.

"A rain check on the dessert, then?"

Mallory liked the sound of that. It would give her an excuse to contact him again. Another chance to dig for a story that had to be in his past somewhere. "Okay."

Five steps led from the sailboat's deck to the cozy main cabin that was filled with the amenities Logan had mentioned. The small kitchen area boasted a sink, cooktop, oven, microwave and wood cabinetry that deserved points for both function and form. Upholstered benches flanked a table on the opposite wall. Further back was a comfortable seating area and a door that she guessed led to a bedroom, since the bathroom's door was clearly marked with the word Head.

"This is nice," she commented.

She meant it. Mallory didn't know much about sailing. For that matter, she'd never been inside a boat like this one. But the glossy hardwood and soft-hued fabrics and upholstery were homey and inviting. The gentle swaying motion didn't hurt, either.

"I like it."

"This is an older boat, right?"

"She dates to the 1970s," he agreed.

"She." Her lips twisted.

Logan was grinning when he took the dishes from her hands and set them in the sink. "I'm guessing you consider it sexist that boats are referred to using female pronouns."

"Not sexist necessarily. Just…annoying."

"Right. From now on I'll call my boat Bob," he dead-panned. "Better?"

"I don't know." She shrugged. "He seems more like a Duke. Besides, it has a name."

"Tangled Sheets." He grinned and she fought the urge to fan herself.

"That's an interesting name for a boat. One might even call it a bit risqué."

"Why? A sheet is another name for a sail, Mallory." His face was the picture of innocence now, but it was plain he understood the double entendre because when he turned to retrieve two coffee cups from a cupboard the grin returned.

"Well, someone has either taken excellent care of this boat or it's been restored."

"The latter," Logan confirmed. Over his shoulder, he asked, "Cream or sugar?"

"Black."

He handed her a steaming cup and poured one for himself. Leaning back against the sink, he said, "It took me an entire winter's worth of weekends after I purchased her—" he cleared his throat "—I mean, Duke, to finish the overhaul. I basically gutted the place and started over. And I'm still puttering most weekends."

He glanced around the salon and nodded. Puttering

still or not, his expression made it clear he was pleased with his progress so far. Mallory could understand why. Logan might not look like the sort of man who would know a hammer from a ham sandwich, but obviously he could hold his own with the guys on HGTV. Power suits and power tools didn't normally go together. Questions bubbled.

"Where did you learn carpentry and—" she motioned with her hand "—how to do repair and maintenance?"

"One of my dad's hobbies is woodworking, and he's always been good at home repair. My brother and I spent a lot of time with him in his workshop, helping him put things together. I picked up a few tips along the way."

"I guess *so.*"

"You're surprised."

"Maybe a little. You don't look like the sort of man who would be…"

"Good with his hands?" he finished.

He set his coffee aside and held up both hands palm side out. His fingers were long, elegant, but the palms were calloused. The man was definitely hard to figure out, but she wasn't trying at the moment. She was staring at those work-roughened hands and wondering how they would feel…on her skin.

Mallory swallowed and ordered herself to stay focused. "Why not just buy something brand-new?"

"I don't know. I guess you could say I prefer a challenge."

The way his eyes lit made Mallory wonder if that was what he considered her to be.

Logan was saying, "Besides, she had great bones and an even better history. Her previous owner had sailed her from Massachusetts all the way to Saint Thomas the year before I got her and nearly lost her to a hurricane along the way."

"So, your boat is a survivor and you had a hand in resurrecting her…him."

"Duke."

"Duke," she repeated.

His laughter was dry. "Yes, but I can assure you I don't suffer from a God complex."

"Then why did you get into psychiatry? Didn't you want to save people?"

"I wanted to *help* people." Oddly, he frowned after saying so. He sipped his coffee. The frown was gone when he added, "Most people have the tools to turn their lives around all on their own. They just need a little guidance recognizing those tools and learning how to use them."

"Good analogy. I guess you really are the son of a carpenter."

"Yeah." He laughed and was once again his sexy self when he asked, "Ready for that sail?"

"Of course. That's why I came."

CHAPTER THREE

LOGAN used the motor to maneuver the boat out of its slip at the yacht club. Once away from the shore, he cut the engine and enlisted Mallory to help him hoist the sails. He could have done it by himself. That's what he usually did, even though it was a lot of work for one person and took some of the pleasure out of the pastime.

Pleasure.

That's what he was experiencing now as he and Mallory stood together on the deck while the boat sliced neatly through the water. He rarely shared *Tangled Sheets* with anyone. It was his private retreat, his getaway from not only the hustle of the city, but from the fame he'd chased so successfully and the reporters who now chased him. Reporters who were much less dangerous than Mallory Stevens was…at least to hear his agent tell it. Nina Lowman had made Logan promise to call him later in the evening, apparently as proof that he'd survived the encounter. Even so, he didn't regret his decision to ask Mallory aboard.

He attributed the invitation to the fact that he'd been

without the company of a woman for several months. Scratch that. He'd been without the company of an *interesting* woman for several months, maybe even for several years. Logan's last fling, and *fling* was almost too generous a term for it, had been with a socialite who'd turned out to be every bit as vapid and vacant as she was gorgeous. Tonya may have been stimulating in many regards, but conversation wasn't one of them. Logan enjoyed smart women. He enjoyed savvy women. Women who were as adept at playing chess as they were strip poker. Logan would bet his last stitch of clothing that Mallory could hold her own in both games.

So it really was no surprise he was enjoying himself this evening. The bonus was that the feeling appeared to be mutual. Glancing over, he noticed that Mallory was leaning against the rail. Her eyes were closed, and the fine line between her brows had disappeared. Even with her face turned to the wind, a smile tugged at the corners of her lips.

For the first time since he'd met her, she looked truly relaxed. And all the more lovely for it, which was saying a lot. The woman was naturally beautiful to begin with: fresh-faced, unmade, unpretentiously pretty. Of course, she could afford to have a light hand with makeup. Her lashes were dark and ridiculously thick and long. They fringed a set of eyes that were rich with secrets. No other adornment was necessary.

A man could get sucked into those eyes if he wasn't careful. It was a good thing Logan had no intention of being lulled into complacency, even if he did enjoy the challenge of staying one step ahead of her.

The eyes in question opened. If Mallory was unnerved to find him studying her, it didn't show. She regarded him in return—boldly, bluntly and not the least bit embarrassed or uncomfortable. Logan swallowed, experiencing again that low tug of interest that seemed to define the time he spent in her presence.

"I probably should apologize for staring," he admitted. He waited a beat before adding, "And if you were another kind of woman, I would."

Her brows rose fractionally. "Another kind of woman?"

"The coy sort."

"Coy." Her lips pursed. "That's not a word one hears often nowadays. It's rather old-fashioned."

"Exactly."

"I'm not old-fashioned."

No, indeed. Mallory was worldly, at least in the sense that she grasped nuances, gestures. She wasn't hard, though. He recalled the way she'd looked when speaking about her parents' divorce. Then she had seemed almost vulnerable.

"Nor am I coy," she continued now.

It was impossible to tell from her tone whether she was insulted or not. Logan decided she wasn't. "Which is why I don't feel the need to stand on pretense around you. I can say what I mean."

"Hmm." It was an arousing sound that drew his gaze to her mouth. "Is that a good thing or a bad thing?" she asked. When he glanced up and met her gaze, the amusement shimmering in her eyes told him she'd already made up her mind.

"A good thing. Definitely a good thing."

She laughed. The sound was low and throaty. "I don't know. I think I might prefer some pretense every now and then. I get so little of it. Subterfuge, sure." She exhaled. "That's par for the course in my line of work."

"But we're not talking about your work." Interesting, Logan thought, how it kept coming back to that. Interesting and a little unnerving.

Mallory smiled. "Oh, that's right. We're talking about pretense."

Not just talking about it, he thought. Well, two could play the game. Logan decided to up the ante. "Are you saying you *want* me to pretend that I don't find you as sexy as hell?"

She blinked. He'd caught her off guard. He'd done it a few times in their relatively short acquaintance. Perhaps it was his male ego talking, but he liked knowing he could manage it.

"Well?" he prodded when she remained quiet.

"I'm trying to think of a response."

"And you can't?" That came as a surprise.

Mallory cleared her throat. "Well, you have to admit, Doc, yours is a loaded question."

Just the sort of question she was very good at asking, but he kept the observation to himself. Instead, Logan snorted. "And here I thought you weren't one to act coy."

"Well, if I tell you no, you'll think I'm playing games, but if I say yes, you'll accuse me of being vain."

"Will I?"

She ignored his question. "You've painted me into a corner. I don't like corners."

"Sorry. I didn't realize."

"Yes, you did."

He flashed a grin. "Okay, maybe I did. But in my defense, I find myself immensely curious as to what your answer will be."

The wind tugged at her hair, sending several strands of it across her face. Mallory pushed them aside with the palm of her hand. The gesture was practical and… "Tell me, Doc, what woman doesn't enjoy being called sexy?"

It was a question rather than an actual answer, but Logan let it pass.

"For the record, I believe I said 'sexy as hell.' If you're going to quote me…" He left the sentence unfinished in part because the words were unnecessary, but mostly because her complexion paled. When she stumbled back a step, he reached out to steady her. "Mallory? Are you all right?"

"Fine." She moved back another step to lean against the rail, forcing him to release her arm. "I…I guess I don't have my sea legs yet." He didn't think that was what had caused her momentary weakness, but she was saying, "In response to your finding me 'sexy as hell,' what am I supposed to do?"

"I have a couple of suggestions." He bobbed his

brows to lighten the moment and was rewarded with a laugh.

"I hate to break it to you, but *coy* isn't another word for *promiscuous*."

Logan snapped his fingers in a show of disappointment. "Damn."

"You know, if I thought you really meant that, I'd have to toss you overboard."

He had little doubt she would try and perhaps even succeed despite the fact she was no match for him physically. "How would you get back to the yacht club then?"

She folded her arms across her chest. "Oh, I'd manage."

Even from their short acquaintance, Logan could tell that about her. Mallory was a survivor. That caused him to sober. He'd met survivors before. He'd counseled a good number of them in his private practice before he'd taken his profession to the airwaves. While he admired their ability to persevere and overcome, in some cases survivors could be very solitary. They didn't need anyone.

"It's time to head back."

"Already? You know, I was just kidding about leaving you bobbing in Lake Michigan." She laughed again.

Logan joined in. "I know."

"But I've made you nervous." The line returned between her brows.

"Not because of that remark," he admitted.

"Hmm." There was that sexy sound again.

"There's not much daylight left and I'm not a fan of

sailing in the dark. Besides, I have some prep work to finish for tomorrow morning's show." It wasn't a complete fabrication. In addition to taking listeners' calls, Logan included a segment on general mental-health topics. Tomorrow's, appropriately enough, was panic attacks.

He prepared to bring the boat around. Mallory helped. In fact, she insisted on lending a hand, as if it was vital that she know what to do to return to the safety of the shore. Survivor, he thought again.

"Watch for the boom," he called. "Or you'll be the one overboard."

"Aye-aye," she called, offering a salute even as she ducked to avoid being struck.

When the Chicago skyline with the sun peeking around the skyscrapers was before them, she whistled. "Talk about a million-dollar view."

"It's something all right. Want to take a turn at the helm?"

"Are you kidding?"

"I never kid when it comes to my boat."

"Then, yes." She stepped into place, legs splayed shoulder width apart, hands at the ten and two positions on the wooden wheel he'd spent hours sanding and staining. Though there was no need, Logan moved in behind her and set his hands over hers.

"Don't you trust me?" she asked.

"Sure." He dipped his head low enough so his jaw scraped her cheek and whispered into her ear, "I'm just looking for a good excuse to touch you."

Was that a shiver he felt? It was hard to say since Mallory's voice sounded perfectly normal when she asked, "Do you need an excuse to do that?"

"Apparently."

"Sad." She made a tsking sound. "Perhaps you should see someone about your…hang-up around competent women."

"Hang-up?"

She shrugged. "I know this famous doctor who might be able to offer some advice."

"Really?" He let his cheek brush against hers. "Should I make an appointment?"

"No. He's much too busy to take appointments these days. Famous, remember?"

"Ah. Right."

"But you could place a call to his radio program. It airs weekday mornings, top of the FM dial. All of Chi-town tunes in to listen to it."

"Don't forget the rest of the greater metropolitan area," he added.

"How could I? He's the savior of their maddening morning commute. Who knows how many cases of road rage he's nipped in the bud with his calming words of wisdom. Hundreds would be my guess."

"I'd venture thousands," Logan said. "No wonder he's said to be in contract negotiations for a nationally syndicated television show."

Mallory went still. The teasing humor was gone from her tone when she said, "Really?"

God, was the woman ever off the clock? "That's the rumor, anyway. Sadly, it's unconfirmed."

Logan felt a little guilty for baiting Mallory until she leaned back against his chest. Then he just felt…her. More precisely, he felt the vibration of her laughter. "Well, I'm sure the doctor can help you."

Dark hair tickled his jaw. "Why are you sure?"

"From the press releases I've read on this guy, he can all but walk on water."

He'd seen those releases, which had come courtesy of his agent and the station's marketing team. He knew what Mallory meant. The accolades were true but they made him uneasy, for the very fact that while he'd once believed he truly had a gift for helping people, these days he sometimes felt all he did was entertain them for a few hours of product-sponsored programming.

"What if the renowned Dr. Bartholomew is just a man?" he asked quietly.

"Just a man?"

"Human," Logan clarified.

"Are you saying he's fallible?"

"Would that be so hard to believe?"

Mallory laughed again. "After reading those press releases, yes."

"Forget what you've read," he said seriously. "Make up your own mind."

She turned halfway around, bracketed in his arms, her lithe body trapped between his larger, harder one and the wheel. The late-day sun sparked off the highlights in her hair and turned her eyes ethereal. "I always make up my own mind, Logan."

"I'm glad to hear it."

The moment stretched as they regarded each other. Something flickered in her gaze. He needed to believe it was the same damnable attraction he was suffering. When Logan finally managed to drag his gaze away, it came as a surprise to realize they were almost back at the yacht club.

"We need to lower the sails," he said, backing away.

"Timing is everything," he thought he heard her say.

Once they were docked, Logan helped Mallory step onto the wooden planks. She didn't require assistance. Come right down to it, she was the sort of woman who would never require assistance, or at least never ask for it. But he wanted to touch her and was pleased when she took the hand he offered.

It was odd to be saying goodbye on a dock. Logan was the sort of man who walked a woman to her door. Mallory might not be old-fashioned, but he found he still wanted to and he said as much.

"That's all right. I got here under my own steam."

"But the El? This time of night. If you wait, I can drive you home."

"I don't mind the El. Don't worry about me. I can make it to my apartment alone." She tilted her head to one side. "But, thanks. Your offer is…sweet."

"And no less than you deserve," he said.

"Yeah." She tucked some hair behind one ear. Flattered? Shaken? "Well, thank you for this evening.

Dinner was excellent and the sail was an experience I won't soon forget."

"Glad to hear it."

She motioned beyond him to where the setting sun played peekaboo around the skyscrapers. "I like the city. I love it, in fact. I think I feed off its endless energy." She laughed. "But tonight…I didn't expect to enjoy being away from it as much as I did, being able to see it, yet remain separate."

He knew exactly what she meant. "You're welcome."

She smiled and backed up, offering a little wave. "Good night, Logan."

"Good night." Part of him didn't want the evening to end. When she started to turn, he called out, "I'd like to see you again."

That stopped her. "You would?" The line deepened between her brows, even though she grinned. "To keep an enemy close?"

Logan didn't smile. "No."

"Then why?" Her head angled in challenge.

The ball was in his court. He was grimly serious when he said, "Because of this."

He closed the distance between them as he spoke and pulled her into his arms before he could think better of it. His mouth found hers before she could mount a protest. He should have known Mallory wouldn't protest. Hadn't they already established that she wasn't coy? Instead, she rose on tiptoe and boldly kissed him back. When he would have ended it, she was just getting started, tilting her head in the opposite direction and deepening the contact.

Zip. Zap. Zing. He dove back in.

The woman might well be the death of him, but Logan didn't care. He hadn't felt this alive in years.

CHAPTER FOUR

THE encounter with Logan played on Mallory's mind as she waited for her train to arrive. Actually, it more than played on her mind. It obliterated all other thoughts.

The man sure knew how to kiss.

But then, she'd expected more than mere competency from someone who looked like Logan. What she hadn't expected were fireworks. These weren't some piddling display, either, but the kind that lit up the sky for a citywide Independence Day celebration. God help her, they were still going off, raining down sparks on her heated skin, especially when she recalled the wanton way in which she'd responded to him.

She'd wrapped her arms around him, clinging like some sort of human ivy.

The man was a story, she reminded herself yet again. Dinner and an evening sail on his boat had been borderline unprofessional, but Mallory had bypassed her conscience, telling herself she was meeting him in the name of research. Research didn't include getting physical. She'd crossed the line big-time with that kiss.

Though the sun had set, the temperature hadn't dipped much, and she was too keyed up to go home, where her air-conditioning was on the blink. There was no way she wanted to sit alone in her hot little box of an apartment and ruminate about Logan's masterful mouth and her appalling lack of restraint and professionalism. She opted to return to the office.

This wasn't the first evening that had found Mallory in the *Herald*'s multistoried Art Deco building on Grand Avenue. She'd been known to sleep on the lumpy sofa in the women's lounge when a story kept her late. When she entered the lobby this evening, the second-shift security guard smiled and sent her a friendly wave.

"Hey, kiddo."

Kiddo. Sometimes Mallory felt positively ancient despite not having yet reached her thirtieth birthday. Tonight was one such time.

"Hi, Joe."

"Cubs are up by three runs in the bottom of the seventh," he informed her as she waited for the elevator to arrive. "A win tonight will put them three games ahead of the Sox."

"I'm not switching my allegiance," she said of her beloved baseball team. She'd been a fan even before moving to Chicago, which was one of only a couple cities to have more than one Major League franchise. "Even if my guys wind up dead last and the Cubs go all the way to the World Series, you won't find me cheering them on. There's still such a thing as loyalty, you know."

The older man merely winked. "You'll come around, kiddo."

"Not in this lifetime," she replied as she stepped into the lift.

Relative silence greeted Mallory when she stepped off on the fourth floor. The *Herald* was an afternoon paper, which meant it went to press before noon. At this time of the evening only a couple of overnight city desk editors and a smattering of reporters, including the one working the night-cops beat, were at their desks. The television was on, tuned to a cable news channel, and static-laced conversations could be heard coming from the omnipresent police scanner. She breathed in the earthy scent of newsprint and the underlying odor of stale cigarette smoke. Smoking had been banned building wide a few years earlier, but even a fresh coat of paint on the walls and new carpet tiles on the floor hadn't managed to completely banish the smell.

Careers had been made in this newsroom. Mallory would be damned if she would give up hers without a fight.

Pushing Logan's kiss to the recesses of her mind, she grabbed a bottle of diet cola from the cafeteria vending machine and headed to the second-floor library. In newspaper jargon the library was also known as the morgue. It was as quiet as one tonight when she flipped on the overhead lights and stepped inside.

These days technology made it possible to access every story, photo and caption that ran in each day's edition from the computer at her desk, which was one of the reasons the library's staff of six had been pared down to two, one of whom worked only part-time. The computer system had been in place for a while now, but everything that predated it was stored in this room, either on microfilm or in individual files of clippings that were categorized by both the reporter's byline and the story's subject matter.

Mallory started with the clip files, grabbing a handful by a senior lifestyles reporter who'd covered the city's social scene at the *Herald* for more than three decades. Logan was a born and bred Chicagoan, and his wealthy parents regularly made headlines for charity work and other good deeds. Maybe, just maybe, she'd get lucky.

Two hours later Mallory rubbed her bleary eyes and finished off the last of her now warm diet cola. She'd gone back through several years' worth of clippings and had found nothing more controversial than a photograph of his father christening a sightseeing boat for a company that was the top competitor of one that now regularly advertised on Logan's program.

She was ready to call it a night when she spied a folder titled Engagement Announcements that had accidentally been filed with the other. A light bulb clicked on. Logan wasn't married now, but had he ever been?

Her question was answered forty-five minutes later when she opened a folded yellow clipping that announced the engagement of Logan Reed Bartholomew and Felicia Ann Gable. He was nearly a decade younger in the photo, but he looked the same even though his hair was a little longer and his face less angular. The woman standing at his side smiled adoringly at him. She also was stunning and Mallory's polar opposite with long blond hair and classical features.

Mallory's stomach knotted. She passed it off as excitement though it felt suspiciously like disappointment or, more ominously, dread. But that was ridiculous. She *wanted* to find dirt. That's why she was in the newspaper's morgue scouring clip files for leads. It was why she'd accepted Logan's invitation for dinner and a sail. Of course, the fact he had been married wasn't exactly dirt. His wife could have died. Or he could be divorced. A lot of marriages failed. Statistically speaking, half of them, as her mother liked to remind her. Divorce wasn't a story…unless it was the result of something serious such as spousal abuse or some kind of addiction.

Logan an abuser…either of women or substances? That didn't seem possible. But during her years of reporting, Mallory had encountered people every bit as seemingly upstanding as Logan with even darker secrets to hide.

"A fall wedding is planned," the notice read.

"Now we're getting somewhere," she murmured half under her breath.

From a filing cabinet at the back of the room she pulled out a stack of files of wedding announcements starting in late September of the same year and running through March of the following one. Sometimes it took newlyweds months to turn in the notice, especially if they were waiting to receive proofs from their photographers.

She'd just settled back in her seat when the door opened.

Sandra Hutchens eyed Mallory in surprise. "You're here kind of late, aren't you, Stevens? Or has another screw-up caused you to be busted back to night file clerk?"

"Funny," Mallory muttered between gritted teeth. "What are you doing here?"

"Gathering a little background for an investigative piece I'm working on with Tom Gerard." Tom was one of the reporters assigned to district court. "You remember those?"

Did she ever. God, she missed real news.

"All the Freedom of Information Act requests we had to file are finally paying off. Heads are going to roll after this story runs."

It was all Mallory could do not to salivate, especially since she knew her demotion was the only reason a hack like Sandra was now working on such a meaty story with Tom.

"Enjoy it while it lasts," Mallory muttered, knowing an explanation of "it" was unnecessary.

Sandra grinned. "Oh, I intend to."

It was all Mallory could do not to snarl. She and Sandra tolerated each other in a professional setting, but it was an open secret that no love was lost between them. Their adversarial relationship dated to Mallory's days as an unpaid intern at the paper. Sandra, who had been at the *Herald* for nearly a decade by that time, had covered Chicago government, and she'd balked at having to take a rookie around on her beat. Not long after, that "rookie" had made a fool of her.

After a seemingly mundane city council meeting, they had returned to the newsroom where Sandra had filed a straightforward story about the city not renewing its contract with the current waste management company. Mallory, however, had acted on a hunch and done a little more digging.

Two months later, her piece exposing a scandal involving three aldermen receiving kickbacks from the new firm ran across the top of page one. Then it was picked up by the Associated Press wire service and printed in newspapers from coast to coast. Sandra had hated Mallory ever since, and she had celebrated Mallory's fall from grace by buying a round of drinks for patrons at the Torch, a hole-in-wall pub that catered to reporters and other working stiffs rather than tourists.

"Wedding announcements." Sandra's eyes narrowed. "What are you up to?"

"You know those fluff pieces we get to do for the Lifestyles section," Mallory evaded. "Who cares what styles of dress were in fashion a decade ago?"

Sandra snorted out a laugh. "Wedding fashions. My how the mighty have fallen."

Offering a brittle smile, Mallory rose to her feet and raked the files into a pile, intending to leave.

Sandra laid a hand on her arm. "Have you filled out the form to check those out?"

"I'm just taking them to my desk." Actually, Mallory

was planning to take them home. Per usual, she had no other plans for the weekend.

"It doesn't matter. If you're taking clip files out of this room, you need to fill out a form," the other woman insisted and pointed to the stack of papers on a high counter next to the door.

Mallory snorted. "Right. And you do that every single time you walk out of here with clips."

"No." Sandra's smile was smug. "But we're not talking about me. We're talking about you. And for someone who's basically on probation, I'd think you'd be eager to follow the rules."

"How kind of you to remind me of that," Mallory muttered.

"Don't mention it." She smirked. "Really, it's my pleasure."

Mallory filled out the necessary form, jotting down the file numbers, the date and, because she was feeling peevish, she put Sandra's name down as the person checking them out.

Logan's apartment was quiet when he arrived home. He'd loitered on his boat for a couple of hours after Mallory left, thinking as much as puttering. As he'd washed the dinner dishes, stowed the small barbecue grill in the hold and checked the rigging, he'd tried to figure out what his next move with Mallory should be.

He still hadn't reached a conclusion, though he knew he shouldn't have kissed her. Hell, even as he'd drawn her into his arms, he'd known that. But just as he hadn't been able to resist the temptation she'd posed then, he couldn't muster any regret now.

At home he prowled his penthouse, which offered stunning views of the lake from the living room's large windows and a generously proportioned patio. Where once he'd welcomed the high-rise's solitude and privacy, it just seemed lonely now. He poured himself a drink and headed outside.

Part of him had hoped that whatever magic spell Mallory had cast on him would wear off with that kiss. It hadn't and the other half of him was damned relieved. Despite all of his uncertainty, one thing was clear: tonight wasn't the end of it.

The phone on the bedside table rang before eight the following morning. Logan grabbed for it, muttering a sleepy hello even as he folded the other arm over his eyes to block the light coming from the window.

"You didn't call last night," the woman on the other end of the line accused without the courtesy of a greeting.

"Sorry." Squinting, he levered up on one elbow, more amused than irritated. "Am I grounded?"

His agent dismissed the teasing question with an audible huff. "What happened with Mallory Stevens? I want to know everything."

That statement cut deeply into amusement's lead over irritation. "I don't believe in kissing and telling."

Logan regretted the words instantly.

"Dear God!" Nina exclaimed. "Please tell me nothing happened between the two of you."

"Nothing happened," he repeated in monotone.

"This isn't funny, Logan."

"No, it's not." But Nina failed to detect the edge in his voice.

"You can't trust her," she went on. "Reporters like her are sharks. They get one whiff of blood in the water and they go on the attack."

"That's rather dramatic," he drawled. "Besides, I thought you said Mallory was a pit bull? Sharks and dogs are two different species, you know."

"Logan—"

He sat up fully and swung his legs over the side of the bed. "Look, Nina, as touching as I find your concern, my personal life is just that…personal."

"I guarantee you that Mallory doesn't see it the same way. If she finds out something about you that can help sell newspapers, she's going to use it. And unless it's out and out false and maliciously published, we won't be able to do a damned thing about it because you're a public figure."

His agent was right, of course. As a celebrity, he was fair game. If Mallory sniffed out a story, she would write it. What did it say about him that he didn't care? Besides, he rationalized, what did he have to hide?

So he told his agent, "There's no need to worry. She's curious about the syndication deal. She's not the only reporter who is."

Maybe he would give her an exclusive when the terms of the contract had been hammered out.

"In the meantime," he continued, "there's nothing Mallory Stevens is going to discover about me personally that's exciting enough to grace the front page of her newspaper or any other. As much as I hate to admit it, Nina, my life is pretty damned pedestrian."

"Are you sure about that?"

"I'm positive."

CHAPTER FIVE

NOTHING.

After scouring the clip files that was exactly what Mallory had found. She'd even returned to the newspaper morgue late Saturday for wedding announcements through the end of that calendar year. Again she came up empty-handed. Even if Logan and Felicia's planned fall wedding had wound up delayed for several months—and why would that happen?—no record of it appeared in the *Herald*.

Record or no record, something told Mallory she was on the right track. She decided to press on. Monday morning, between writing advances for a couple of alternative-art exhibits, she searched the state's vital records for a certificate of marriage. *Nada.* If the couple had married, they had not done so in the state of Illinois.

On a hunch, Mallory checked the records for Felicia's name alone. *Bingo!*

She could have saved herself a lot of time and effort if she'd done so first, she realized. Miss Felicia Ann Gable had been a fall bride after all. She'd wed another man, Nigel Paul Getty. The nuptials were performed by a justice of the peace. This probably explained why no wedding announcement had appeared in the newspaper. When a bride threw over her groom for another man just before they were to say I do, flaunting it in the media was bad form.

Poor Logan.

The sympathy Mallory felt for him far outpaced her excitement over the discovery. She told herself it was because she didn't yet know if this lead would pan out. Besides, she knew how it felt to find out your significant other was cheating. Two years post-Vince, Mallory still felt like a fool for not having put two and two together sooner. It would have helped her save face among their mutual friends, many of whom apparently were privy to the fact he was two-timing.

Her telephone rang as she mulled over what to do next. "Mallory Stevens," she said distractedly into the receiver.

"Just the person I was hoping to reach."

The aggrieved groom in question was on the other end of the line. Mallory stared at the photograph of his lovely former fiancée, feeling oddly guilty and fighting the urge to apologize.

"Logan, hi. What…why are you calling?"

"I need a favor," he replied.

"What sort of favor?"

"I've been invited to a dinner this Thursday evening at the Cumberland Hotel. It's a benefit to raise funds to send children with life-threatening illnesses to summer camp."

"And you're hoping to get a mention of it in the *Herald*," she guessed.

"Actually, I was hoping you'd agree to come with me." He chuckled dryly. "Good cause notwithstanding, these things can be tedious."

"You want me to go with you," she repeated in surprise.

"Not interested?"

"I didn't say that."

"No. But neither have you said yes," Logan pointed out.

"Yes." Even though Mallory had spent the weekend reminding herself of ethical boundaries and the danger of mixing business with pleasure, the answer slipped easily from her lips.

"Terrific. Dinner is at seven with cocktails and appetizers starting at six. Would five-thirty be too early for me to come by and collect you?"

She'd have to leave work a bit before her usual quitting time to reach her apartment and be ready on time, but she didn't hesitate before saying, "That's fine."

"Good. And, Mallory?"

"Yes?"

"I'm looking forward to it."

She pictured him grinning and her skin grew warm. Despite all of her internal lectures to focus and be professional, Mallory knew Logan wasn't the only one filled with anticipation.

* * *

Between Monday and Thursday, Mallory put in more than a dozen hours fleshing out what she knew about Logan's failed relationship. Felicia not only had hurriedly remarried, she'd moved out of state a few months later. She and her husband relocated to Portland, Oregon, where they'd had a son, who was either premature or conceived before they were wed. This, Mallory figured, was the reason for Felicia's defection.

A year after that, Felicia and Nigel Getty were divorced. These days, Felicia was a businesswoman, though perhaps not for much longer. Barring an infusion of cash, her upscale fragrance boutique would soon be in Chapter Eleven.

What went around came around.

Thursday started out bad and continued downhill for the rest of the day. Mallory forgot to set her alarm clock, missed her El train and then spilled half of her first cup of coffee down the leg of her ecru trousers while waiting for the next one. Unfortunately, she had no time to return home to change clothes, so she arrived at the *Herald* wearing spotted pants that smelled like Arabica beans.

As Mallory slunk to her desk, Ruth Winslow, the Lifestyles section editor glanced up from her computer and then consulted the large wall clock.

"I wasn't aware you had an interview this morning," Ruth remarked.

"I didn't. My alarm clock…" Ruth's steel-colored eyebrows rose, cutting off the rest of Mallory's explanation. "Sorry."

"I'll expect a list of story ideas by noon for the special

pullout tab on street festivals that's going to run next Sunday, and I've got a couple of advances for you to write. I need both by the end of the day."

"Sure." Now would not be a good time to ask to leave early, Mallory decided.

When Mallory spilled a second cup of coffee on her clothes half an hour later, she began to wonder if Logan's ex wasn't the only one getting smacked by karma.

Given the way her day had gone, she didn't find it surprising that she was running late. Logan was leaning against her apartment door when she arrived home.

"Have you been here long?" she asked as she balanced her oversize shoulder bag on one knee and dug through it for her keys.

"Fifteen minutes or so."

Mallory glanced up and winced. "Sorry."

He cast a considering look. "That's all right. I'm guessing you've had a bad day."

"That obvious?"

A smile played around the corners of his mouth. "Let's just say your clothes tell a story."

When her fingers wrapped around the keys, she sighed. "They only offer the abridged version, believe me. I felt like the poster child for Murphy's Law today."

"Sorry to hear that. If you want to cancel, I'll understand."

As tempting as she found his offer, she waved it aside. "That's kind of you, but no. Of course, if a natural disaster strikes while we're out tonight don't say that I didn't give you fair warning."

"I won't," he replied on a laugh.

Mallory opened the door and invited Logan inside, grateful that the place looked presentable. Housework tended to rank low on her list of priorities, especially when she was in hot pursuit of a story.

"I have a decent bottle of Merlot in the kitchen if you'd care for a glass while I'm getting ready," she told him as she toed off her shoes.

"Should I pour some for you?"

She sent him a wry look. "Given my track record today with beverages that stain, I think I'd better pass."

Mallory's apartment was small, easily a third the size of Logan's condo, but glancing around, he decided it offered a huge insight into the woman. Her music collection included CDs by Duke Ellington, Miles Davis and Fats Waller, making her a fan of jazz. The bold red wall that served as a backdrop for a piece of oversize geometric art said she wasn't afraid of color. And her eclectic sense of style—Asian-inspired pieces were mixed in with a boxy modern couch and more traditional leather recliner—told him she didn't believe in following someone else's rules.

She also liked to read. A built-in bookshelf to the left of the television boasted lengthy tomes by some of the country's leading political commentators, classic literature by the likes of E. M. Forster, William Faulkner and Sylvia Plath, as well as the newest thriller from Tami Hoag. There were no self-help books, he noted, unless he lumped the one on basic home repair into that category. No surprise there. Mallory was self-reliant, self-sufficient.

A survivor.

When the uncertainty he'd experienced on his sailboat niggled again, Logan decided to take her up on the offer of wine.

Her kitchen wasn't much bigger than the galley on his boat, but since Mallory had already admitted she didn't cook, he doubted she thought it deficient. He found a corkscrew in one of the drawers and located a wineglass in a top cupboard. As he sipped Merlot, he glanced at the snapshots and other clutter stuck to the front of her refrigerator. One in particular caught his attention. It was of Mallory and another young woman. They were sitting on a split-rail fence wearing cowboy hats and silly grins. Mountains peaked in the background, making it clear the photo had not been taken locally. A vacation? Whatever the occasion, she looked so open and uncalculating. No questions to be asked. No agenda.

Would she ever be that way around him?

"That's my college roommate, Vicki."

Logan turned at the sound of Mallory's voice and nearly fumbled his wine at the vision that greeted him. "Roommate?" he managed.

"Yes. She lives in Chicago, too, and we've remained close since graduation. Once a year she talks me into going on some wild adventure. She claims it's good for me."

"I think I like her already."

"Last year, it was working a cattle drive. That picture was taken before our first grueling day in the saddle. Hence our smiles."

She motioned toward the photograph, but Logan's gaze was taking in the pale-gold cocktail dress she wore. Cap sleeves showed off a pair of toned arms and a short hem highlighted her killer legs. The flirty jeweled sandals on her feet caught the light and shot off sparks.

Logan swore he felt some of them land on him.

"You look amazing."

It was no empty compliment he paid. In the amount of time it took most of the women he knew to apply their makeup, Mallory had changed clothes, done something sexy with her hair and added a bit of drama to her eyes. She was pretty before, lovely. She was dangerously gorgeous now, and he wasn't sure whether he should be grateful or nervous.

"Thanks."

"I'll be the envy of every man there." He meant that, too. Her unconventional looks turned heads even when she wasn't also wearing something sexy.

Mallory brushed the compliment aside. "Let's not get carried away."

Because he wasn't a man given to hyperbole, Logan persisted. "You're gorgeous."

"I'm not." She expelled a breath, not so much exasperated as flustered, which he found interesting, endearing.

"Who told you that?" he asked.

Her brows beetled. "No one told me that. I'm not

fishing for a compliment here. I'm not ugly. I'd even go so far as to say I'm attractive. But gorgeous? No."

"Why?" he countered.

"I have a mirror."

Logan didn't care for her explanation. Generally speaking, Mallory didn't suffer from low self-esteem. Hell, he'd never met a more confident, self-possessed woman…when it came to her profession. But someone definitely had made her feel lacking when it came to her appearance. Who? Why? The answers would have to wait. But this couldn't.

"Then you must not look in it very often." He took her by the shoulders and steered her to the foyer, where an oval-shaped one hung on the wall over a small table that was stacked with junk mail. "See?"

Mallory studied herself for a moment, but then offered a dismissive shrug. "I'll have to take your word for it."

"Will you?"

This time it was his reflection she surveyed. Logan let his hands slide from her shoulders to her hands, releasing one so he could turn her around.

"Well?"

She leaned forward slightly before stepping away. "We'd better get going. We're already late for your party."

"Fashionably so," he assured her, even though generally speaking Logan was a stickler for punctuality. "A few more minutes won't hurt."

But she shook her head. "I just need to go grab my

handbag and a shawl. You go on ahead. I'll meet you downstairs."

Logan was still standing in the foyer when she returned from her bedroom. After taking the gauzy wrap from her hands and settling it around her shoulders, he took her arm and escorted her downstairs to his waiting car.

The hotel's ballroom was crowded with people—entrepreneurs, politicians, celebrities and members of Chicago's social elite. Some had come out to support a worthy cause. Others had come out to be *seen* supporting a worthy cause. Mallory recognized many of them, including the alderman who was rumored to be taking bribes from a development firm. Another time she would have been tempted to corner him and ask a few questions to see what she could get him to say on the record. This evening, however, the only person she found herself curious about was Logan...and it had nothing to do with a story.

He looked incredible. No surprise there, of course. The man not only could afford to wear Armani, his broad shoulders and lean, muscular build did the suit justice. But there was more to Logan than Hollywood good looks. She'd never doubted his intelligence, but he was deeper and far more complex than she'd first realized.

He fascinated her not because she was a reporter, but because she was a woman.

Gorgeous? Did he really think so? And those manners of his, opening doors, helping her with her shawl. He made her feel as if she'd just fallen into a fairy tale.

"Mallory?"

She blinked, becoming aware that the man in question had been speaking to her while she'd been gazing at him. She could only hope she wasn't wearing some sappy expression on her face.

"Sorry. My mind strayed."

"And here I thought you were hanging on my every word," he teased. "I was just saying that the seating isn't assigned. Do you have a preference?"

She glanced around. At this point all of the tables had at least two or more occupants, which meant introductions would be necessary, small talk, too. Usually she enjoyed meeting new people. As for small talk, Mallory was good at it, and even better at getting folks to open up about themselves. But suddenly she didn't want to socialize or chat or look for possible stories. She wanted to be alone with Logan, picking up where they'd left off in her foyer.

"Would you mind sitting at a table near the back of the ballroom?" she asked.

His brows notched up at the suggestion. "So we can leave early without causing much of a disturbance?"

"Exactly."

When he smiled, it caused another sort of disturbance, especially when he asked Mallory, "Am I to assume you have something in mind for us later?"

"Maybe," she allowed.

What was she getting herself into? She didn't know. She didn't care, which was totally unlike her.

She was off her game completely, she realized a moment later when she failed to notice Sandra Hutchens until it was too late to avoid her.

"Hello, Mallory. I wondered who was here for the *Herald*."

The other woman's gloating snarl turned to bewilderment, however, the moment she recognized Mallory's escort.

"You're…aren't you…?"

"Yes." Logan took the hand Sandra was pointing in his direction and shook it politely. "I'm Logan Bartholomew. And you are?"

"A pain in my butt," Mallory muttered at the same time Sandra gave her name.

"Mallory and I work together."

"Are you here covering the benefit?" Logan asked, unaware—or was he?—of how insulting the senior reporter found the question.

"No. I have a beat that allows me to write actual news stories." Sandra sniffed. Her gaze shifted to Mallory then, and the malicious triumph in her expression was impossible to miss. "I'm here tonight as the guest of Larry Byram. You remember him, don't you Mallory."

Oh, she remembered Larry, all right. Her teeth clenched. Larry was one of the mayor's top aides and the weasel who'd fed Mallory the bogus story and quotes that ultimately had led to her demise.

"How is Larry?" she asked sweetly.

"He's good. And enjoying a promotion."

No doubt he was also enjoying Mallory's demotion. "How nice for him," she managed.

"I'll tell him you said hello," Sandra offered with ill-concealed delight.

"Yes, please do."

"Would you excuse us for just a moment?" Sandra said to Logan. She grabbed Mallory's arm and dragged her a couple of feet away without waiting for his reply. "I don't know what you're up to, Stevens," she hissed the moment they were out of earshot.

"Up to?"

"Don't play games with me. You're with Logan Bartholomew."

"I know."

"Why?"

"I should think that's obvious."

"Not in your case," Sandra snapped. "You don't have a real social life, so I know whatever is going on between you two has got to be work related."

She wanted to deny it and was a little troubled that she couldn't, not completely. "Your point?"

"Unless it's something an intern could write in her sleep, *you* shouldn't be working on it."

"What? Are you my editor now?" Mallory asked. "If so, I missed the memo."

"Leave the real stories to those who can do them without costing the newspaper a bundle."

Sandra's remark posted a direct hit. Mallory felt her

face heat, partly from irritation but mostly from embarrassment. She couldn't prove it, but she knew she'd
been set up. Still, it was her own fault. Even if she was
able to return to her beat eventually, would she ever be
able to live down her costly mistake?

"I've got to go."

When she attempted to walk past Sandra, the other
woman blocked her path and pointed a finger in her
face. "Just so you know, I'm watching you. One more
screw-up and you'll be gone."

"You'd like that, wouldn't you?"

"I live for the day."

Mallory managed to sound bored when she said,
"Then you need to get a life, Sandra."

"Charming woman," Logan remarked when Mallory
rejoined him.

"Yes, we're the best of friends."

"As tight as Brutus and Caesar, I'd say."

"Exactly, which is why I watch my back whenever
she's around."

"How about if I keep an eye on your back…and other
things…tonight?"

His brows lifted and so did the pall the encounter
with Sandra had cast over Mallory's mood.

"I see a table over there." She pointed to one that was
adjacent to a side entrance.

"Good choice," he replied, nodding toward the doors.

"I thought so."

She changed her mind a moment later. Two other
couples already were seated there sipping cocktails and

sharing a plate of appetizers. Introductions were made, although both of the women knew Logan—or, rather, knew who he was—even before he gave his name.

So much for Mallory's hope that the two of them could just chat between themselves until the opportunity to leave arrived.

"Oh, my God! You're Logan Bartholomew! *The* Logan Bartholomew!" the bustier of the two brunettes shouted. "I just love your show. I listen to it every morning while I'm getting ready for work."

"Thank you."

"My name is Anita, by the way. And this is my husband, Victor."

"It's nice to meet you, Anita." Logan turned to shake Victor's hand. "And you, too."

"The same," Victor replied, although he didn't appear to be nearly as starstruck as his wife.

"I feel like I already know you." When Anita winked flirtatiously, Mallory gritted her teeth, feeling oddly possessive.

The other brunette piped up then. "I'm your biggest fan, Dr. Bartholomew. I never miss your show."

"Please, it's just Logan."

"Logan." She actually giggled. "I'm Julia Richmond." Motioning to the irritated-looking man sitting beside her, she added, "Thanks to you, Darin and I have been able to work out some of our differences and keep our relationship moving forward. We're getting married in the fall."

She extended her left hand, showing off a diamond

engagement ring big enough that it should have required an escort of armed guards.

"Wow," Mallory said. "That's some rock."

"Tell me about it," Darin muttered.

Logan cleared his throat and offered a diplomatic "Congratulations to you both."

"Thanks. We owe it all to you, don't we, honey?" Julia wrapped an arm around Darin, who said nothing. Instead, he hoisted his drink in a mock toast and took a liberal swig. Mallory gave their marriage a year, tops, assuming they even made it to the nuptials, which at this point looked dicey.

Julia was saying, "The advice you give on your show, especially to couples who are having problems, is right on the money. It's like you wrote the book on relationships or something."

"Yes. You're very insightful, especially when it comes to understanding women and what we need from the men in our lives," Anita chimed in.

Darin wasn't the only one who looked irritated now. A muscle had begun to twitch in Victor's jaw. It was clear neither man appreciated the attention Logan was receiving. Mallory wasn't thrilled with it, either.

"I'm glad you found something I've said to be of help," he replied modestly.

Far from basking in the women's profuse praise, Logan shifted uncomfortably in his seat. And no wonder, given his personal history, Mallory thought. If he'd written the manual on relationships, as Anita claimed, he wouldn't have been blind-sided by his fiancée's infidelity and virtually left at the altar.

Mallory decided it was time to steer the conversation to a neutral topic.

"So, how 'bout those White Sox last night?" she said, earning black looks from the women and a sneer from Darin, who was obviously a Cubs fan.

Logan, however, latched on to the new subject. "Did you see that play at third base in the bottom of the seventh inning?"

Because she could tell that all of his enthusiasm wasn't manufactured, Mallory grinned. A Sox man. Who knew? Another reason to like him.

"See it? I screamed so loud I woke up half my building. Detroit thought they had the game sewed up till that play, then our boys rallied," she said with the kind of pride only other diehard fans could understand.

Victor apparently was one of them. Either that or he was just eager to talk about something other than relationships. He began rattling off the standings for the teams in the American League Central. Darin entered the discussion a moment later and for the next several minutes a spirited debate on the designated-hitter rule ensued. Anita and Julia didn't look all that pleased that sports were now dominating the conversation, but they began to chat between themselves about Julia's upcoming wedding, so all was well. Beneath the table, Mallory felt Logan's hand brush her knee. When she glanced over, he mouthed the word "Thanks."

"No problem," she mouthed back.

Several minutes later, Buck Warren, the head of the charity, took to the podium to welcome everyone and thank them for coming. He also made a not-so-subtle request for donations with the reminder that such gifts were tax deductible. Afterward, dinner was served. No rubber chicken, thank goodness, but Mallory couldn't help thinking the pork tenderloin was on the dry side and the steamed green beans were undercooked.

"They should hire you," she informed Logan after washing down a bite of the tenderloin with some wine.

He shrugged off the compliment. "It's easier to cook dinner for two than it is for two hundred."

"True. I wonder what the dessert will be. I hope it's chocolate."

He leaned over and whispered, "In the mood for a little decadence tonight?"

"As a matter of fact…" Heat shimmied up her spine as she returned his smile.

Dessert turned out to be apple pie with a side of vanilla ice cream that came largely melted.

"How disappointed are you?" Logan asked.

"Very." But something occurred to her then. "You know, this might be a good time to claim my rain check."

"You want me to make you dessert?"

She nodded. "Something with a sinful amount of chocolate in it. What do you say?"

"And leave before the dancing even starts?" He looked comically appalled.

Chocolate was momentarily forgotten. "You dance?"

"Slow only. I made a point of learning how in junior high school when I figured out it was a good excuse to put my arms around a girl without getting smacked for my trouble."

"Very calculating." But she laughed. "Well, we have to stay now."

"Eager to be in my arms?"

Though she was, she said, "I'm more eager to find out how good you are." When his brows rose, Mallory added dryly, "At dancing."

A local band had been hired for the event. Its female singer was dressed in a vintage floor-length gown, her hairstyle reminiscent of something from the 1940s. Mallory almost expected to hear "Boogie Woogie Bugle Boy" when the band started its first tune, but the song turned out to be a modern ballad. The small dance floor filled up quickly. Even so, Logan rose from his seat and held out one hand.

His lips were twitching, but his eyes glittered with a dare when he asked, "Shall we?"

"Oh, by all means."

Their hands remained clasped as they weaved their way through the tables to the dance floor. Even that minor bit of physical contact had Mallory's hormones starting to hop and hum. When they reached their destination and he pulled her into his arms, it was all she could do not to moan. Their bodies bumped, separated and brushed, but only occasionally as they swayed and circled to the music. Mallory forgot about moaning. Now she wanted to scream with need. The eagerness

Logan had spoken of earlier mocked her now. She was pretty sure he knew it, too.

He dipped his head lower. "Mmm. You smell good." The words vibrated against her ear.

"So do you." Though, of her five senses, touch was the one she was focusing on now. She turned her head slightly and their cheeks collided.

"Mmm," he said again.

"The song is almost over." And with it this sweet torture would end.

"I know. But there's still dessert."

"Yeah." She sighed. Her mouth was watering, though the hunger she hoped to satisfy had nothing to do with food.

"Do you have something in particular in mind?" he asked.

"You're open to requests?"

"Always and especially from you."

She smiled. "I'll have to think about it. Maybe you can tell me what your specialties are."

"Sure. I'll list them after we leave. But I'm open to trying new things, too."

"In the kitchen," she clarified.

"Right. In the kitchen." He nibbled her neck. "That's where I do my best cooking."

"Yeah?"

His hand stroked her lower back, causing her to tremble. "I'll show you."

"Mmm. Looking forward to it," she said.

The music stopped. The floor began to clear.

"Want to stay out here for another dance?" Logan asked.

"I'd rather go."

"Okay." His hand found the small of her back as they started for their seats.

"Home," Mallory added.

He stopped walking, turned toward her. His slow, conspiratorial smile further stirred her agitated hormones.

CHAPTER SIX

LOGAN drove the speed limit and took a detour after leaving the party, trying to give both of them time to come to their senses. They couldn't do this.

Well, they could, obviously, and he figured with mutually satisfying results. But they shouldn't.

His body demanded a reason why not. Unfortunately, he was damned if he could come up with one. Still, he was sure one existed. Probably several, for that matter. His agent could tell him, but he wasn't interested in calling Nina Lowman right now.

That's when he realized it. He didn't want reasons. He didn't want to come to his senses. He wanted this night with this woman. If there were consequences to be paid afterward, he'd pay them. With interest if need be. But tonight, even if just for tonight, she would be his.

He depressed the accelerator and the car shot forward. Mallory glanced sideways at him. God help him, he thought he saw her smile.

He'd planned to take her to his penthouse. He had

a spacious bedroom, including a king-size bed. Given the way he felt, extra room seemed a good idea. But as he moved through traffic, accelerating through yellow lights, he decided against it. Her place made more sense.

First of all, taking her to the condo seemed too presumptuous, even though the signals she'd given off all evening pretty well confirmed they were on the same wavelength. Secondly, it wouldn't allow either one of them a graceful out if they changed their mind. A doubtful scenario, that. But still. And third, it would save him from having to run her home in the wee hours of the morning.

Yeah, the conclusion that their lovemaking would last for hours was presumptuous, too, but surely one primal encounter wouldn't be enough.

He pulled to a stop outside her building, lucky enough to find a parking space, although at this point he would have left his car in the fire lane if necessary.

"Well, here we are." It was all he could do to keep from thumping his head on the steering wheel after making that hackneyed observation. Worse than sounding eager, he sounded nervous. And he was. He was hardly an inexperienced teenager, but his hormones didn't seem to know that. He felt eager and nervous and, hell, just plain desperate. God help him, his palms were even damp.

In the dim light of the car's interior, he thought he saw Mallory's lips twitch.

"Yep. Here we are." He heard the latch on her seat

belt unhitch. "You're coming up, right? I have that wine. It seems a shame to drink a glass alone."

"Well, in that case…"

Mallory was apprehensive, though need trumped her nerves. It was obvious Logan felt the same. Gone was his sexy swagger and confident radio voice. Out of the corner of her eye, she saw him rub his palm on the leg of his trousers before taking her hand. Even so, it felt hot to the touch and telltale moist. She found his sudden lack of polish endearing and every bit of a turn-on as the way he'd held her in his arms when they'd danced earlier.

At her apartment door, she handed him the key, which she'd thought to have out in advance. Since he seemed to like doing these small courteous things, she would let him. Truth was, she liked his manners.

The apartment was dark and quiet, though she thought she could hear her heart beating. She hadn't left a light on. She walked to the lamp on the table next to the couch and switched it on.

"So, some wine?" she inquired.

He was still standing just inside the door. "If you're having some."

"You're not worried about driving, are you?" She raised one eyebrow in subtle challenge.

"Should I be?" The corner of his mouth lifted.

"No." But then Mallory shrugged. "Although I have heard that even small amounts can impair one's ability to drive…among other things."

Logan crossed to where she stood. "Then I shouldn't chance it. I want to be fully…able."

His hands found her hips and he pulled her into closer proximity. As his head dipped low, she whispered, "I'd prefer that as well."

He bypassed her mouth and started with her neck. The first nibble sent a series of shocks through her system.

Zip, zap, zing.

She enjoyed every one of them, no longer trying to determine why she felt the way she did. Some things defied explanation.

"Mmm." The sound vibrated out on a moan.

"You like that?"

Logan's voice had taken on a cocky air. Apparently he'd found his footing again. She didn't know whether to be glad or disappointed. Glad, she decided when his mouth began to explore the other side of her neck.

"You have to ask?"

"Not really."

Cocky, definitely. It was time to level the playing field. She backed up a step, creating just enough distance between their bodies that he was forced to stop exploring her collarbone. He looked at her in question.

"I probably shouldn't tell you this, but whenever we're together, I get this…this sensation."

"Sensation?"

"Uh-huh." She nodded solemnly.

"Really? Where?"

"I don't know if I should say."

"You can tell me," he coaxed.

"That's right. You're a doctor." Mallory's smile was bold. He returned it in kind.

"Exactly," Logan told her.

"It starts about here." She laid her right hand on her chest.

"Here?" His fingertips skimmed her exposed collarbone in a sensual caress.

"A little lower, actually," she managed in a voice that verged on studious.

"Lower?"

"Yes."

"Hmm." His gaze turned from considering to smoldering as his hand slowly meandered south, where it kneaded the upper curve of her breast through the satiny fabric of the cocktail dress.

"Here?" he asked.

"Still lower," she managed. This time her voice was a breathy whisper. She decided to show him rather than use words. Placing her hand over his, she guided it down until the fullest part of her breast filled his palm. "Right here."

His head dipped down and he whispered her name against her cheek as his hand's gentle movement had her knees threatening to buckle. But she wasn't through.

"That's where it starts, Doctor. But that's only where it starts."

Mallory thought she heard Logan swallow, though it was hard to tell over the loud thudding of her heart. As for her, she had nothing to swallow. Her mouth had gone dry. So much for leveling the playing field.

"Where does it end?" he asked.

She should have been nervous. She had been. Now, she was anything but. She felt powerful, empowered. For the first time in her life, she knew exactly what she wanted and it had nothing to do with news beats or stories or journalism awards.

"Let me show you." She took his hand and turned, pulling him in the direction she wanted to take him. The direction she wanted to go, despite the lines that would be crossed on the way to her final destination.

Logan glanced past her to the hallway that led to her bedroom. He didn't move and she was forced to stop, as well. "Are you sure, Mallory?" His hand squeezed hers. "I want you to be sure."

Mallory swallowed. Something inside of her warmed. Logan was ever the gentleman, even at a time like this. He really was a special, special man.

I'm positive, she thought, but what she told him was, "If you want to find out exactly how sure I am, you'll have to come with me."

Logan stayed the night. The *entire* night. Leaving just after dawn the next morning with his suit coat slung over one arm, his tie peeking out of his trouser pocket, stubble shading his jaw and a smile of satisfaction lifting the corners of his mouth.

"I've got to go."

"Me, too," Mallory said. She couldn't afford to be

late to work for the second time in two days, not with Ruth watching the clock and Sandra gunning for her back.

"Bye."

"Bye."

Even so, they lingered in the doorway of her apartment for another fifteen minutes kissing farewell.

"I'll call you later today," Logan said when they finally broke apart.

He did, though it was much, much later.

Mallory scrubbed off her makeup and brushed her teeth, going about her nighttime routine as if nothing had happened when in fact nothing was the same. Her well-ordered world had rocked on its axis.

She had been able to think of nothing else all day except for Logan…and last night.

What a night it had been. It wasn't only what had transpired in her bedroom that had her mind straying from work all day. She couldn't stop recalling the hours that had led up to it.

She kept trying to pinpoint the moment everything had changed. It was the look, she decided. The look on Logan's face when he'd turned around in her tiny kitchen to find her dressed and ready for their evening out. His reaction had made her knees weak.

Mallory still couldn't believe that he thought she was gorgeous. Pretty? Oh, sure. She'd been called that on occasion. More often than not, though, with her oversize eyes and blunt chin, she'd been labeled cute. Add in her personality, especially while on assignment, and *ruthless* was the adjective that most often had been hurled. She'd taken it as a compliment, though obviously the sources who'd issued it hadn't intended it that way.

But *gorgeous*?

She stared at her reflection now, both amazed and intrigued that Logan could see her that way. She'd barely managed to wrap her mind around the compliment when he'd all but seduced her while they'd circled the crowded dance floor. To be fair—and Mallory was a firm believer in fairness—she'd been only too happy to return the favor. And later she had.

She dabbed moisturizer on her face and, rubbing it in, sighed. He'd said he would call today, but he hadn't. Not while she'd been at work, not on her cell phone and not since she'd been home. It was now past eleven o'clock, the last hour of the day ticking away. She tried to remain optimistic, which was something in itself. Even two years into her relationship with her last boyfriend, Mallory had taken every vow Vince made with a grain of salt:

"The next time my boss invites everyone out to dinner, I'll invite you along." "When my parents come to town next time, I'll introduce you." "I've got a buddy who says he'll get us some prime Sox seats for the next game."

Yeah, right. Whatever. Mallory hadn't pinned her hopes on any of her ex's promises. She'd known he would break them. Just as when she was a kid she'd known her father would fail to honor his word the few times he'd actually made plans to visit with her after the divorce.

For reasons she couldn't quite comprehend, she wanted to believe Logan. She didn't want him to disappoint her.

She moved to her bedroom, where she slipped into a tank top and boxer shorts. Pulling back the comforter on the antique four-poster she'd purchased at an estate sale in Lake Forest, she knew there would be no need for down tonight. Even the cotton sheet would be overkill. The air-conditioning unit had been fixed, but even with it blasting on high her skin felt heated.

She was fanning herself and considering a cold shower when the telephone rang. Even before she glimpsed the Caller ID readout she knew who it was. Her heart did a crazy thump and she was glad no one was around to see her foolish smile.

"I was just thinking about you," she said in lieu of the standard greeting.

"I guess that means I didn't wake you. Are you in bed?" His voice was low and all the sexier for it as he asked the question.

"As a matter of fact, I just climbed under the covers." Mallory lowered herself onto the mattress as she made the claim.

"Imagine that. So am I."

Her already elevated body temperature shot to the combustible range as she pictured Logan stretched out on his mattress wearing what he'd had on late last night…nothing. "Mmm."

"What was that?" he asked.

"Nothing." She smiled at the memory. "Nothing at all."

"I'm sorry to call you so late. It was a crazy day. After my show I spent a few hours taping promotional spots to run during other programs and then…it doesn't matter. Suffice it to say it was a really long and tedious day."

"Sorry. We can talk tomorrow if you'd like. For that matter, you needn't have called at all." Though she was so glad he had.

"I told you I'd call. I'm a man of my word."

Logan said it simply, stating it as fact. Her heart did that funny thump thing again. She wasn't sure which she found more disconcerting, the flash of fire he could provoke with a look or this new physical reaction.

"I like knowing that you try to keep your promises," she admitted.

"Everyone should."

"But everyone doesn't."

"You've been hurt," he said.

"Haven't we all?" Mallory waited a beat, wondering if he might mention his own breakup, and not just because she wanted a story and still smelled one here. But because she wanted to know more about Logan for herself.

He made a sound of agreement, but didn't expound on it. Instead he said, "It's pretty much a given that by the time you get to our age someone will have broken your heart or breached your trust. It's the human condition. Of course, that doesn't make it hurt any less."

"No."

She heard him sigh. "It's late. I should let you go."

"Is that a polite way of telling me I need my beauty sleep?" Mallory asked lightly.

"No. You're already gorgeous. Remember?"

Thump!

"So you say." She wrapped her free arm around her middle, hugging herself in an attempt to keep the pleasure his words generated from escaping.

"Still don't believe me." It wasn't a question. "I guess I'll just have to keep telling you until you become a believer."

Because she could think of nothing to say to that, she changed the subject. "What time do you need to be at the radio station?"

"I usually try to get there about an hour before I go on the air." Which meant he would be getting up in about five hours, given his commute. "What about you? What time do you have to be at the *Herald*?"

There had been a time in the not-so-distant past when Mallory had beaten in the copy editors, who were traditionally among the first to arrive in the newsroom. She'd stayed late in the day, too. A fifteen-hour shift wasn't an anomaly, even when she'd had nothing more pressing to do than scroll the national news wires and read the stories. She'd considered it a badge of honor then, a display of her dedication. It seemed a little pathetic now.

"My start time varies depending on what I'm covering. These days, though, it's a pretty safe bet I don't need to be at my desk till eight. You know, about the time the lonely and unemployed start phoning your show," she finished on a laugh.

"They need help, too."

Something in Logan's tone prompted Mallory to ask, "Is this how you expected your life to turn out when you graduated from medical school?"

"No."

Silence stretched after his startlingly candid answer. The reporter in her would have pounced on it, following up his admission with half a dozen questions intended to reveal more. But all Mallory said was, "I'm sorry."

More silence ensued. When she could stand it no longer, she said, "Logan? Are you there?"

"Yeah. I'm here."

"We're off the record, you know," she felt the need to point out. "It's just the two of us…talking."

"The two of us." He still sounded doubtful.

And though part of her wasn't sure it was the wisest course to take, she further clarified, "Just a man and a woman. Not a potential story and the reporter interested in writing it."

"Really?"

"Really."

"What I just said could make one hell of a story, especially with a nationally syndicated television talk show in the works." He swore ripely after the words slipped out.

Another exclusive gem and Mallory was privy to it.

But what she asked was, "Have you talked to anyone about this?"

He laughed. "Do you mean a professional? Now that would put your byline on the *Herald*'s front page. Chicago's Doctor-in-the-Know seeks counseling over career crisis."

His comment stung, but even more so, she felt for him. Here was a man who helped thousands with his advice, yet he had nowhere to turn when he needed guidance.

"You know, I'm here if you ever need someone to talk to, Logan. I'm not sure what kind of advice I can offer. Helping people is a little beyond my degree. But I'm a pretty good listener," she added. "Even when the content of the conversation isn't for publication."

"You really mean that."

"Yeah."

"Thanks." He laughed then, though without much humor. "I still can't believe I told you that."

"Because I'm a reporter?" Mallory asked, the lead weight returning to her stomach.

"No. Because I've never so much as hinted about that to my folks. They're usually the first people I go to when I need to hash things out."

What a luxury, she thought, to have parents you could confide in and seek counsel from. "Why haven't you said something to them, then?" she asked.

"I don't know. I guess I haven't wanted to worry them. Besides, they're so proud of me."

"But you have to be proud of yourself," she said

softly. "You have to be happy doing what you're doing or their pride won't matter."

Soft laughter filtered through the line. "And you said you're not good at this. Maybe you could take a turn guest hosting my show."

"Nah. Not my thing." She kicked the sheet to the bottom of the mattress. She was alone in bed, and yet she couldn't think of a more intimate conversation she'd shared with a man while being horizontal. Heaven knew, last night the pair of them hadn't spent much time talking. "Logan?"

"Yeah?"

She felt so privileged that he'd told her what he had, and she was determined to show him his trust wasn't misplaced. "Let's make things even between us."

"What do you mean?" he inquired on a sleepy yawn.

"Ask me anything you want to know."

"Anything?"

He didn't sound sleepy now. Indeed, his probing tone raised gooseflesh on Mallory's skin despite the Chicago night's sweltering heat.

"Yes. Anything."

"Okay." He made a humming noise, apparently considering his options. But he didn't keep her in suspense for long. "Tell me something about you that no one knows."

"No one?"

"A deep, dark secret. That will make us even."

"Something no one else knows," she repeated, thinking. The memory came, rising up from the recesses of her mind with all the unpleasantness of bile. As such, it nearly gagged her. For a moment she considered telling Logan something else. But honesty demanded honesty. She swallowed and began.

"I told you that I hadn't seen my dad since my parents divorced. But that's not true. I ran into him a few years ago."

"In Chicago?"

"Yes. Well, sort of. We were at O'Hare. I'd been out of town covering a story for the newspaper and I'd just returned home when I spotted him in the baggage claim area at the airport."

She squeezed her eyes closed, girded her heart. Not that any measure she took did any good. The pain trickled through her system as painful as acid. Three years had passed, but the memory remained fresh. The wound was still festering.

"And?" Logan prompted when she said nothing more.

"He looked the same as I remembered." She cleared her throat, hoping to make her voice sound more nonchalant. "He had a little more gray at his temples and a few more inches around his waist, but overall he was exactly the same. Tall and imposing and looking like he'd rather be anywhere but the place he was."

She remembered that look well. He'd worn it during holiday gatherings, during her dance recitals, on those few evenings when he'd been home and she'd asked him to read stories.

Mallory had to swallow again before she could

continue. "I saw him, and even with thirty feet and half a dozen people between us, I knew him at a glance. I guess I must have changed a lot, though."

"He didn't recognize you," Logan guessed.

"No." It was worse than that, though. "Actually, he thought I was a porter."

"Aw, Mallory."

"After I tapped on his shoulder, he turned and smiled. But before I could even say, 'Hi, Dad,' he handed me a couple of bucks and pointed to his bags." What started as a laugh ended in a sob. "He expected me to load them on the cart I'd just rented for my own luggage."

"What did you do?"

Even after three years, shame washed through her. Thankfully, anger followed swiftly on its heels. "I should have told him to go to hell, but I was a little too stunned."

"He deserved no less, you know." Logan said it with such conviction that it lessened some of her remaining heartache.

"He had three bags, two of them well over the weight limit. Mom always said he didn't know how to pack light. You know, in addition to being a lousy father, that day he proved he's also a lousy tipper. Three stinking bucks." She snorted. "He should have paid me triple that for the near hernia I suffered."

"Did you ever tell him who you were?" Logan asked.

"Nah." Though Logan wasn't there to see her, Mallory shook her head. "It was too humiliating, especially since I'd already loaded his luggage and he'd handed me the tip."

"What about your mother? Did you tell her?" he asked.

"And give Maude another reason to gripe to me about him? Nah." Mallory ran a hand over her cheeks, surprised to find them damp from tears. She hadn't cried over her father in years, not even after the O'Hare incident. She hadn't thought herself capable of tears any longer where the man was concerned.

"You chose to protect her," Logan said.

She didn't view her actions as altruistic. "He did it to me, Logan. He didn't do it to my mom."

"But she would have commiserated and understood."

"No. Our relationship isn't like that. My mother never would have let me hear the end of it."

"I'm sorry." After a moment of silence, he added, "Thanks for sharing that."

"You know, it felt good," she admitted. "Maybe there's something to therapy."

"I'm not sure I'd classify this as an actual session," Logan began. "But it felt good to tell you what I did, too." He snorted out a laugh then. "And it was a good reminder, too, since I'm always telling my listeners that it's not healthy to bottle up their emotions."

"Do as I say, not as I do?"

"I guess you're right." His tone was rueful. "But no longer. Nothing gets resolved that way."

"You have to face things, don't you?" she said.

"Yes. You do."

Cradling the phone to her ear, Mallory rolled to her side and caught sight of the clock. "Oh, my God, Logan. It's nearly one o'clock."

"I know."

"I really should let you get some sleep."

"I'm not tired. If you hang up now, I'll just lie here awake." She heard his breath hiss through the line a moment before he asked, "Stay with me, Mallory?"

"Okay. I won't go anywhere." Cradling the phone to her ear, she turned on her side, and though he was far away, she felt him beside her, filling up a vast emptiness she hadn't even been aware existed.

CHAPTER SEVEN

MALLORY wasn't sure how she would feel during her next face-to-face encounter with Logan. Excited? Embarrassed? Both? She'd bared her body to him and then a little bit of her soul. They'd spent two nights together, and though miles had separated them during the second one, it had been every bit as intimate as the first. She'd never felt closer to anyone than she'd been with him during those long hours they'd spent talking in hushed tones and sharing secrets until just before the morning sun turned the horizon pink.

When it came right down to it, she and Logan barely knew each other. Yet he already seemed to understand her far better than anyone else. And that was why she knew a moment of uncertainty the following afternoon when she spied him standing outside the *Herald* as she walked out the building's grand front entrance.

"Hello, Mallory."

"Logan."

The strap of the bag carrying her laptop slipped down

her arm. The computer would have crashed to the sidewalk had he not rushed forward to grab it.

She tried to keep a foolish smile corralled as she inquired, "What are you doing here?"

"Besides rescuing your computer, you mean?"

"Yeah, besides that. Thanks, by the way."

"You're welcome." When she held out her hand for the heavy bag, he looped the strap over his shoulder instead. "I wanted to see you."

That foolish smile unfurled. She ducked her head in an effort to get it under control.

"I probably should have called, rather than just showing up at your workplace."

"I don't mind. It's a nice surprise."

"Do you have any plans for this evening?"

She didn't, but even if she had, they would have escaped her now. She couldn't seem to think when he was looking at her like that, all interested and sexy.

"None that I can think of. Why?"

"Good. I thought I'd take you to a jazz club."

Though she couldn't have said why, that brought Mallory up short. "You like jazz?"

"No, but you do. So…" He shrugged, as if that explained everything, and in a way it did.

Heaven help her, Mallory wanted to kiss him right then as they stood on the sidewalk in front of the *Herald*. To hell with the purpose-driven professionals and camera-toting tourists who were streaming around them. She couldn't think of another man—her father included—who'd put what she liked, what she wanted ahead of his own needs or preferences.

"Thank you."

His brow furrowed. "For what?"

"For...the good time I'm going to have this evening," she said. "Would it be okay if we swing by my apartment first so I can change clothes?"

She had on an ivory linen suit that was wrinkled from a full day of wear, and her feet were begging to be freed from a pair of peep-toe pumps that required a little more breaking in to be comfortable. This wasn't what one wore to a club, especially when Logan was clad in denim jeans, Italian loafers and a short-sleeved shirt whose tails he'd left untucked.

"No problem, though I really like those heels. They do sinful things for your legs." He took a step toward her, close enough that there was no mistaking the interest brewing in his eyes.

"You think so?"

"Oh, yeah."

The outside world melted away, just as it had when they'd held each other on the dance floor...and later in her apartment.

"Then you should see me in stilettos," she announced boldly, bluntly and with just a hint of challenge.

"Something to look forward to." His words and the smoldering expression that accompanied them caused Mallory's breath to catch. "Are you ready?"

"Ready?" The question had her blinking.

"To go." He smiled knowingly. "My car's parked just down the street."

"Lead the way."

The Swing Shop was small, dark and smoky. It drew an eclectic crowd—college students, couples young and old, tourists, suit-wearing businessmen and even interns and residents from the nearby hospital, who were still outfitted in scrubs.

Everyone was equal here. At the French restaurant up the block a discreetly passed tip might garner a better table or less time spent on the waiting list, but at the Swing Shop seating was first-come, first-served. Patrons who hoped to get a table came early, often right from work when their day ended. And they tended to stay late, buying drinks and ordering the kitchen's greasy offerings as their feet tapped and their bodies swayed to wailing saxophones and weeping coronets.

Yes, getting a seat was tricky, but a little aggressive maneuvering through the crowd helped. That's why as soon as Mallory spied an older couple rising from a table near the stage, she elbowed her way past two legal-eagle types and a plus-size woman wearing an I Love Chicago T-shirt to plant her beer on the scuffed Formica. Logan caught up with her a couple of minutes and half a dozen *pardon-me*s later.

"That was amazing." He lowered himself into the chair opposite hers. "Professional football players running for a game-winning touchdown could take tips from you."

Mallory merely shrugged. "You know the saying—he who hesitates is lost."

He chuckled. "I take it you've been here before."

"This club is one of my favorites."

"And I thought I was going to be treating you to a new experience."

"That's sweet." And it was.

"This is my first time coming here," Logan confessed.

She stifled her laughter. "Yes. I thought that might be the case when you stood at the door and politely held it open for the large party of tourists who entered just behind us." She glanced meaningfully in the direction of a boisterous bunch of middle-aged women who'd pushed together three of the club's highly prized tables to accommodate their party, not all of whom had arrived yet.

"Now that we have a table, do you want to order something to eat?" he asked.

Mallory crinkled her nose. "The food's not really all that good here, but I tell you what, if you can make do with an appetizer or two until the main attraction finishes, dinner will be on me."

"Do I get to pick the place?" His brows bobbed.

"It sounds like you might have somewhere in mind."

"I might." He pulled a plastic-coated menu from between the salt and pepper shakers in the center of the table. After a cursory glance, he asked, "Do nachos work for you?"

Mallory grinned, enjoying the fact that even though

Logan possessed the skill of a gourmet chef, he harbored no prejudice against more pedestrian fare. "Heavy on the jalapeños, hold the onions."

"Got it." He raised his hand to catch the attention of a harried-looking waitress.

They stayed three hours and might have remained longer if Mallory's stomach hadn't protested. She'd switched to coffee after her second glass of wine, since it seemed to be going right to her head. And she couldn't bring herself to eat another bite of nachos. She was already regretting her heavy-on-the-jalapeños request.

Outside, the night air had cooled considerably from the afternoon high temperature of nearly ninety degrees, but with the heat still radiating from the sidewalk, the change was negligible, especially since Mallory was with Logan and even the casual way he clasped her hand in his had her feeling feverish.

"You said something about treating me to a meal," he reminded her as they made their way to his car.

"Yes, I did. What are you in the mood for?" she asked.

He stopped walking, turned and her question took on a whole new meaning.

"You."

Logan released her hand, but only so he could use both of his to frame her face. His hands were big. His palms warm even to her heated skin. Though she was probably being ridiculous, she thought she could feel the calluses he'd earned tending to his boat.

He'd kissed her before, done much more than that.

But each encounter had struck her as something new, unique. As she had before, she lost herself in his embrace, sucked under and in no hurry to resurface.

The kiss might have lasted seconds or it might have lasted several minutes. Mallory had no clue. Slowly she became aware of the traffic passing, of horns blasting in the distance and of snippets of the conversations from the people walking by them.

She was pressed up against Logan, her body flush with his, making her fully aware of his reaction to the contact. His breathing was heavy and ragged. The hands still bracketing her face trembled. Mallory wasn't one given to public displays. She couldn't seem to help herself around Logan.

"Food is the last thing on my mind after that," he murmured. "You?"

"Who needs to eat?"

He chuckled, but then turned serious. "I want you, Mallory."

"That was obvious," she replied. "I want you, too."

Suddenly, though, she wanted more than sex. Though they had been together for barely a handful of dates, she found herself yearning for a long-term, committed relationship. The kind she'd never had with a man. The kind she'd stopped believing in when her father had packed his bags and gone.

"Where is this heading?" The question slipped out before she could stop it.

Logan blinked. In the scant glow of the streetlights she watched his expression turn guarded.

"I'm not sure," he admitted after an excruciatingly long pause. "I like you a lot, Mallory. That much you should know by now. But if you're asking for promises...I don't know that I can make them."

Now or ever? Thankfully she managed to keep that question to herself. She lifted her shoulders in a negligent shrug.

"No need for promises, Logan. This is what it is." She forced herself to smile and added in a seductive whisper, "And I plan to enjoy every moment of it."

She'd hoped that would be the end of it, but now he was frowning. "What exactly *is* this?"

Words were her refuge and, at times, a trusted defense mechanism. They failed Mallory now, though, leaving her to babble incoherently before she finally managed to say, "I don't know, but we're good together."

"The sexual chemistry, you mean?"

"Yes. That's what I mean." Only it wasn't. Not completely. And she couldn't help wondering why that suddenly bothered her so much. "You probably studied stuff like that when you were getting your degree."

Logan massaged his forehead. Not that he could recall, and God knew he was trying to remember. He was a man of science, but some things defied academic explanation. His intense, over-the-top physical reaction to Mallory was one such thing.

He lifted one hand but stopped before his fingers made contact with her cheek. "That's got to be why I haven't been able to get you out of my head."

Her eyes widened and her lips curved. The traces of

vulnerability she'd tried to disguise with bravado vanished. "You haven't been able to get me out of your head?"

"Don't look so damned pleased," he muttered, even though she didn't look pleased. Rather, she appeared to be surprised. And hopeful? "I've never had this response to a woman before."

"Never?" It wasn't only her expression that held bafflement this time. Her tone was ripe with it.

Recalling the way she'd reacted before the charity event when he'd complimented her appearance, Logan gave in to the temptation to touch her and framed her face with his hands. "In addition to thinking you're gorgeous—and don't try to argue with me this time," he added when her mouth opened, presumably to do just that. "I find you incredibly sexy, Mallory."

She didn't argue. She didn't so much as blink, even when he leaned down and kissed her lightly on her lips. She studied him with dark, watchful eyes. The woman who had a well-earned reputation for being shrewd and intuitive only looked vulnerable now.

"Are we going to stand out here on the street all night or are you going to take me home and make love to me?"

Logan chuckled at her question. Okay, maybe she wasn't *completely* vulnerable.

"Let's go."

His car was half a block up the street. With a press of the key fob, the lights flashed and the doors unlocked. When they reached it, Logan opened Mallory's for her, as was his habit. As they drove, she was quiet.

"Is something wrong?" Logan asked.

"No. Not really." She smiled at him. "You're always opening doors for me, even my car door. You're a gentleman."

"My mother's doing."

"Then I like your mother."

His laughter rumbled low. "That makes two of us." He sobered. "You sound surprised, about me being a gentleman, I mean."

"I've never dated anyone quite like you."

"Why?"

His question had her shrugging. "I don't know. I just…haven't."

As Logan maneuvered the car through traffic, he commented, "You know, it's funny how a lot of people confuse basic courtesy with being condescending. I open your door as a sign of respect. I suppose you could do the same for me. Either way, it's not a gesture intended to display dominance."

"No."

He cast a glance sideways when they reached a red light. "You'd be pretty damned hard to dominate, anyway. You're too strong-willed for that and far too outspoken."

She smiled. "Is that how you see me?"

"More or less." Logan nodded. The light changed and he returned his attention to the road. It was a moment before he glanced sideways again and asked, "How do you see yourself?"

"I don't know." She fussed with her hands in her lap.

"But I've been called worse things than strong and outspoken. In fact, I'd consider both as compliments."

"I'm glad. You should. But that's not an answer, Mallory. How do you see yourself?"

She laughed.

"I'm serious. I'd really like to know."

"Okay. I see myself as determined."

"Come on," he challenged. "You can do better than that."

"There's nothing wrong with determination," she returned, sounding slightly defensive.

"You're right. There's nothing wrong with it." God knew, determination was probably what had seen Mallory through her rough childhood and into a much brighter future. "But surely you can come up with more adjectives than that."

"I'm hardworking," she told him.

Logan blew out a breath, unimpressed. "That's just another label for the same thing. Is that the best you can do?"

"It's enough. It should be enough." Her voice rose.

He reached over for one of her hands. "I haven't known you very long, Mallory, and already I see so much more than that. You sell yourself short."

Even in the dimly lit car he could see her throat work. "Well, do tell."

He wasn't offended by her attempt at sarcasm. He squeezed the hand he still held in his. "No. It's for you to see. Not for me to tell you. It won't have the same impact then. And before you accuse me of analyzing you, how about we change the subject?"

"Okay." She blew out a breath, clearly trying to rally. Determined. Yes, she was definitely that. "So, what do you think of jazz?"

"I like it."

"You sound a little surprised."

"I am. Maybe it was the live performance tonight or the company." He flashed her a grin. "But I really enjoyed myself. I may have to go out and buy a jazz CD. Or you could lend me a couple of yours until I'm sure I like the genre?"

"Maybe," she allowed.

They reached her apartment building. Logan found a parking spot half a block past the front entrance and pulled the car to the curb. Switching off the ignition, he turned to her and asked, "So, are you still mad at me?"

"Mad? Why would I be mad?" But she crossed her arms over her chest. He thought he saw a flicker of challenge in her expression.

He played along. Nodding, he said, "You are, but you know, this could be a blessing in disguise."

Mallory's brow crinkled. "How do you figure that, Doc?"

"Everyone knows that make-up sex is the best kind." He waited a moment before bobbing his eyebrows.

Mallory didn't so much as smile.

"You look skeptical."

And a little amused. Her lips had begun to twitch

despite her effort to remain stoic. "I may need some convincing," she said.

Logan opened his car door and came around to her side. As he helped her out, he said, "Come on, then. Let's get started."

CHAPTER EIGHT

"So, who is he?" Vicki Storm asked.

Their drinks, tortilla chips and a bowl of salsa had just arrived at their table at Tia Lenore when Mallory's best friend and former college roommate asked the question. Vicki wasn't one to beat around the bush. It was one of the things Mallory liked about the other woman, but she didn't appreciate it tonight. For reasons she couldn't quite explain, she hadn't told her friend about Logan.

"Who is who?"

"The man who has kept you so busy that you've skipped not one but two of our margarita dates? And tonight doesn't really count as a margarita night, either." Her friend's nose wrinkled. "You're drinking plain old water."

"I didn't feel like tequila tonight." The truth was, salsa was low on her list, too. She'd been battling a bad case of indigestion for the past week.

When silence ensued, Vicki followed up with an impatient, "Well?"

Vicki worked as an interior designer, decorating the palatial penthouses and estates of some of the area's wealthiest people. She was good at her profession. Downright gifted, in fact. But Mallory still thought the woman should have gone into journalism. She'd make one hell of a reporter. Or a formidable interrogator with the Chicago police department.

"His name is Logan, okay?"

"Does he have a last name or is this some sort of kinky Internet thing?"

The moment of truth had arrived. "It's Bartholomew."

"Logan Bartholomew." Her friend's eyes widened then. "As in the hunky radio doctor?"

"That's the one." Mallory couldn't help the smug smile that accompanied her words.

"There's an ad promoting his show at my El stop. Is he as gorgeous in person or was he Photoshopped to male perfection?"

"He's that good-looking." It came out a near sigh.

Vicki whistled between her teeth. "Well, no wonder you've fallen off the radar. When did this happen? How? Where? Why? Etcetera. And don't even think about skimping on the details," her friend warned, taking a chip from the basket in the center of their table to dip in the salsa.

"We've been seeing each other for about six weeks," Mallory began, using her index finger to follow the path of a bead of condensation on the outside of her glass of ice water.

"Uh-oh."

She glanced up sharply. "What?"

"It's serious, isn't it?"

"We're just dating." Mallory attempted a shrug.

Vicki appeared unconvinced. "So, tell me about this famous hunk you're *just* dating."

No doubt her friend was regretting her offer when, half an hour later, Mallory ended her monologue. She hadn't been able to help herself. Nor had she been able to prevent smiling.

It was no surprise when Vicki plunked back in her seat on an oath. "I think I need another drink. I've never heard you go on about a guy the way you do this one."

Mallory folded her arms. "Gee, sorry if I've bored you."

"You know you haven't. Sadly, given the state of my love life lately, listening to yours is more exciting." Her friend sighed again.

"What about that accountant, John?"

"Jerry. And it turns out he's married."

"Sorry, Vicki. Want to talk about it?"

"Thanks, but we'll save my man troubles for another girls' night out. Back to my point. You dated Vince for what, three years?"

"Technically, three and a half," Mallory said, forgoing the salsa to munch on a plain tortilla chip.

"Yet whenever we got together for margaritas and girl talk his name rarely came up in conversation," Vicki pointed out.

"Vince was a jerk," Mallory said succinctly.

"I'm glad you realize that."

"What was to realize? He cheated on me." Four words that said it all but barely scraped the surface of the pain Mallory had experienced when she'd dropped by his apartment unexpectedly one Saturday and had come face-to-face with the half-naked proof of his betrayal.

"Yes, but he was a jerk even before he stepped out," Vicki said. "He was a real pro at putting himself first and you last and getting you to think it was your idea."

If it were anyone but Vicki saying this, Mallory would have felt ashamed. Since it was Vicki, she pulled a face. "I hate it when you're right."

"And I love it that you've finally met a great guy, one who opens car doors for you and takes you to places that he knows will be of interest to you."

"Logan is great. The more time I spend with him…" She shrugged, smiled.

"You're hooked."

Her friend's smug pronouncement had Mallory straightening in her seat. *Hooked* was just another name for a really big emotion. "Oh, no. No, no, no." She shook her head. "I'm not hooked."

Vicki blinked. "What?"

"I can't be hooked."

Her friend's eyes narrowed and her tone took on an edge. "But you said you'd already decided Logan wasn't a potential story."

"I have." Indeed, Mallory had given up on that idea while lying in bed with a telephone receiver tucked under her ear, listening to him talk and giving voice to some of her private demons. "I'll find another way to free myself from pabulum-writing hell."

Then she frowned. Odd, but for weeks now her career had stopped being the center of her existence. She'd been too focused on Logan. Not the man, but the relationship that was developing between them. For her at least, it was moving well beyond the sex.

Sex…for weeks…without interruption from—

Another thought niggled as she contemplated that time frame, and nausea rose up to taunt her. Mallory pressed a hand to one temple. The room seemed to spin. She wished she could blame it on tequila, but she'd sipped nothing stronger than water. And thank God for that, given what she was thinking right now.

"Oh, no," she moaned, and slumped back in her seat.

Vicki's eyes widened. "Mal, you okay? You're as pale as a ghost."

Mallory shook her head. "I'm not okay."

"Are you going to be sick?" Vicki glanced around in a panic for their waitress. "I'll get the check and meet you outside."

"No, no." She waved off the suggestion, though a little fresh air wouldn't have hurt. "I'm not sick, Vicki. I'm… I'm…"

Her friend leaned forward. "You're what, hon?"

Pregnant? In love?

She couldn't bring herself to say either aloud. Instead she murmured, "I think I may be heading toward hooked."

* * *

Later that evening, alone in her apartment, she read the display on the early test kit she'd purchased on the way home. She was indeed going to have a baby. Logan's baby.

Slumping down on the closed lid of the toilet, she let out a long breath. She was scared to death and excited beyond measure.

She'd been physically attracted to Logan from the very start, but she'd suspected for a while now that so much more was at stake. Maybe that was why she hadn't told Vicki or anyone else about the relationship. She hadn't been ready to face what was happening.

Her heart was on the line, the same heart the other men in her life—the really important ones—had made a bad habit of breaking.

Now even more was on the line than that.

How was Logan going to feel when she told him he was going to be a father?

Logan whistled as he wrapped up his work at the radio station for the day. His Doctor-in-the-Know program had ended an hour ago and on a professional high note. For once he'd felt as if he really was doing some good. A caller had complained about her elderly mother's recent odd behavior. Sadly, it sounded like the early signs of dementia, although it could have been a drug interaction or even a vitamin deficiency. Off-air, he'd stayed on the line with her, suggesting a list of questions the woman should ask her mother's doctor.

Perhaps reaching out to people who felt they had

nowhere else to turn for advice was every bit as important as serving clients in a private practice. Perhaps even more so.

All he had to do before leaving for the weekend was finish some paperwork and catch up on correspondence from fans. Logan made a point of clearing his e-mail at the end of each week and selecting a few from listeners who'd been unable to contact him on-air, which he then discussed in his Monday morning "mailbag" segment.

As he sifted through the e-mails, though, his mind was on Mallory. They had plans for the evening. There was nothing especially new in that. They'd spent time together almost every day, meeting for lunch, going out for dinner, taking evening sails on *Tangled Sheets*.

He couldn't seem to get enough of her. He didn't want to. The more time he spent with the woman, the more time he wanted to spend with her. She was one of the most fascinating people he'd ever met. So many damned layers. And he was enjoying peeling back each one to see what was revealed.

His interest was not that of a psychiatrist, though his training made it easier to understand why she could be so confident in some aspects of her life and so utterly vulnerable in others. If he ever met her father—not that it looked like there was much chance of that—Logan was more likely to sock the guy in the jaw than to shake his hand. That was saying a lot, since generally he frowned on violence and considered it a poor substitute for civilized discourse. But give him ten minutes alone with Mitchell Stevens and Logan would put his fists to good use.

Divorce or no divorce, what kind of man walked away from his children and failed to provide for them, not only financially but emotionally? Perhaps because of his own loving upbringing, Logan found it inconceivable and unforgivable. He ached for Mallory and detested the harm such an elemental rejection had done to her psyche. But his interest in her was not that of a doctor or counselor. His interest in Mallory was purely that of a man…a man who was having a damned hard time keeping his hands to himself.

The only stumbling block to total peace of mind was that he didn't quite trust her. Not completely and without reservation. He needed to believe that Mallory's only reason for seeing him was personal. He almost did.

Almost.

His hesitation had less to do with her reputation—which his agent called to remind him of daily—than it did with his past. Nearly a decade after Felicia's bombshell that she'd found someone else and was leaving, his heart finally had healed. It was perfectly whole now, every last fissure mended. Not surprisingly, he wanted to keep it that way. But relationships—the serious and long-term variety, at least—required one to take a risk. Logan wasn't sure he was ready to do so, even if that was exactly what he regularly advised some of his lovelorn callers to do.

Case in point, Emily in Elmhurst, whose e-mail was on his computer screen at the moment.

Dear Doctor,

I've been dating my current boyfriend for nearly a year. I would classify our relationship as serious, though he hasn't mentioned marriage. We are both in our thirties and we both have suffered bad breakups in the past. My concern is this: I have yet to meet his family. They live nearby and he sees them regularly, but I have never been invited along. Could he be trying to tell me something?

"Confront him about the matter, but without hostility. Discuss the situation calmly," Logan wrote. "Your boyfriend may not think the relationship as serious as you do, or it may be something else entirely at the crux of his hesitation. Something such as…"

He frowned at the computer screen as his own experience juxtaposed with that of Emily's beau. He understood the man's hesitation. He understood it perfectly.

Logan hadn't brought a woman around his family since his breakup with Felicia. They had accepted his ex-fiancée, loved her and when she betrayed him, they had felt betrayed, as well. So, just as he'd guarded his own heart these past years, he was careful with theirs.

He was contemplating the wording of his advice to Emily—advice he wasn't sure he would be ready to heed—when his cell phone trilled. It was his brother.

"Finally," Luke groused upon hearing Logan's greeting. "You've been a hard man to reach lately. If it weren't for hearing your voice on the radio, I might think something bad had happened to you."

"Sorry. I got your messages." Luke had left three in the past week. None had seemed urgent, or Logan would have returned them immediately. "I was going to call you today."

"I've tried you day and night. Where have you been?"

"Out."

Logan's monosyllabic response earned laughter from the other end of the line. "No kidding." Luke sobered somewhat when he asked, "Is everything okay?"

"Better than okay, actually."

"Hmm." More laughter followed. "So, what does she look like?"

"Funny," Logan evaded. "Is there a point to this call?"

"Beyond my being concerned about my big brother's welfare, you mean?" Barely fifteen months separated them in age. When they were boys, they'd fought unmercifully. As men, they had become the best of friends.

"Yeah. Beyond that," he said dryly.

"Fine. I need your taste buds. Even though you'll never be able to hold a candle to me in the kitchen, I trust your judgment."

"Gee, thanks." Logan leaned back in his chair and doodled on the edge of the desk blotter with his pen. "For what exactly?"

"I want to expand the Grill's menu," Luke replied, referring to his restaurant. "We offer a terrific selection at lunchtime. The diverse crowd we pull in reflects that.

But traffic falls off significantly in the evening. The same patrons who faithfully come in at noon for our sandwiches, soups and salads, forget all about us when the sun sets."

"Is business bad?" Logan asked. The economy being what it was, a lot of establishments that relied on people's disposable incomes were foundering. If Luke needed cash to see him through to better times, Logan would offer it. No questions asked, no strings attached. They were family.

"I wouldn't classify it as bad," Luke hedged. "We do well enough thanks to eat-in and takeout lunch orders, but I'd be able to make a couple of my servers full-time if we brought in a better dinner crowd."

Logan set his pen aside and rubbed his chin. "So, what kind of dishes are you considering?"

"Nothing five-star."

"You're too casual an establishment for that," Logan agreed, thinking of the Grill's comfortable interior. It boasted no linen tablecloths, chandeliers or fancy flatware, but with its framed vintage posters and brightly colored stoneware plates it was hardly on a par with a fast-food stop.

"Exactly. I have a few pasta dishes that I think would enjoy broad appeal, and I'm toying with the idea of a catch-of-the-day fish special to play off our proximity to the lake."

"That sounds like a good idea. What about chicken or beef?"

"I put smothered chicken on the dinner special board

last week and it did pretty well. Beef?" Luke blew out a breath. "Other than my burgers I'm undecided."

"I've got a couple ideas."

"That's what I was hoping. So, do you think you could sample a few recipes and give me some advice?" Luke asked.

"Sure. Glad to. Just say when and where."

"Tonight at the restaurant. Say around eight. The dinner rush will be done by then."

"Tonight?" Logan's heart sank. He and Mallory had reservations at an exclusive, celebrity chef–owned restaurant. It had taken nearly two weeks to secure them. "I already have plans."

"That's all right," Luke said. No disappointment was audible in his brother's voice.

"I'm glad you understand."

"Oh, sure. No problem. I don't mind if you bring her along. Just make sure she's hungry."

"Luke," Logan began, but he was already talking to a dial tone.

Mallory opened her apartment door that evening wearing a strapless black dress. The satin ribbon spanning her waist made her look like a present—one Logan was eager to unwrap.

After sucking in a breath, he said, "Look at you."

"And look at *you*." Her gaze meandered down. Logan had forgotten all about the jeans and T-shirt he'd thrown on. "It would appear one of us didn't get the memo. The last I heard formal attire was required at Romeo's."

"It is." He winced. "There's been a change in plans. I should have called, but…" He let the words trail off.

Her gaze skittered just to the left of his shoulder. "You're canceling our date," she guessed.

That had been his plan, and he could still do it. Mallory was giving him the out, already expecting him to disappoint her. Had he really thought their trust issues were all one-sided?

"Not exactly."

The line appeared between her eyes as she continued to study the wall. She looked a little pale, he thought. And the vulnerability she tried to hide made an appearance. "What does that mean?"

"I promised my brother I'd come by his restaurant tonight. He's thinking about adding a few new items to his dinner menu and he wants my input." He swallowed hard. Once the invitation was tendered, there would be no going back. Is that what he wanted, for her to meet a member of his family? He answered the question by asking one of her. "Will you come with me?"

Mallory's gaze veered back to his. "Are you sure? I'll understand if you want to go alone."

She would, too. She would understand his defection, because she was so damned used to it. Logan forgot about guarding his own heart. It was hers that required protection.

"Come with me tonight, Mallory." He reached for her hand. "Please. I want you there."

The smile that bloomed on her face was almost his undoing. "Okay. Just let me change my clothes."

CHAPTER NINE

THE Berkley Grill was in a prime location just blocks from Navy Pier. Logan managed to find a parking spot on the street just up from the restaurant. As he escorted Mallory to the door, his nerves jangled. He was anxious about introducing her to his brother. Luke would like her and vice versa, but he hoped neither would read too much into tonight.

One step inside the bustling restaurant and Logan knew his brother had. The Grill was sparse on square footage, sporting no more than twenty tables and half a dozen booths that lined the walls. Almost every seat was filled with diners, including the one just outside the kitchen doors. At it sat his mother, father and sister, Laurel.

God help him. God help him and Mallory both.

He might have been tempted to grab her hand and head back through the door, but his mom was already rising to her feet and waving her arms.

"Logan, over here." Her voice could be heard over the din of conversation and background music.

Mallory glanced at him in question. "It looks like my folks came tonight, too." He had to clear his throat before he could add, "And my sister."

"Apparently your brother wants them to sample some recipes, too."

But her tight smile said she knew better. The Bartholomew clan had gathered to form and offer opinions, but none of them had to do with the Grill's new menu plans.

"If you'd rather not stay, I'll understand," Logan began. "We can stop somewhere else for dinner."

"I have no problem meeting your parents." The line reappeared between her brows then. "But maybe that's not what you mean. Maybe you don't want them to meet me."

"Generally speaking, I don't bring my dates around my family," he admitted, and watched the line deepen into a groove.

"Okay." She started to back toward the door, but he grabbed her hand, tugged her to his side.

"You didn't let me finish. I said, generally speaking I don't introduce the women I date to my family, but I want them to meet you, Mallory."

He watched her swallow. "You do?"

It scared him a bit that he meant it when he replied, "Yes."

The groove disappeared and a smile lit up her eyes. She looked so beautiful just then it was all he could do not to pull her into his arms and kiss her. "I want to meet them, too."

"Good." He squeezed her hand, grinned. "Later, when they're still picking over your bones, remember that I offered you a way out."

"I don't mind questions. I'm a reporter."

"Take notes, then. My mother will make you look like an amateur."

Mallory walked hand in hand with Logan through the restaurant. Outwardly, she knew she looked composed. Inside, she was a quivering bundle of nerves. Logan's family. Was she ready for this? She could only imagine what they were going to think of her.

She swallowed and recalled the photograph of Logan and Felicia. Even in grainy black-and-white the other woman's classical beauty had been undeniable. And her background had been much more in line with the Bartholomews' social standing. Logan insisted that he found Mallory gorgeous, a fact that went a long way toward buoying her confidence now, but she knew she was a diamond in the rough compared to Felicia's highly polished gem. What's more, even though logically she knew no one could tell she was pregnant, Mallory still felt like she had a flashing neon sign on her forehead that read: Expecting.

Mallory had been in the Berkley Grill before, though never in the evening. It was crowded with customers— families, couples, friends out for a quick bite, tourists pouring over El train maps. The only people she was paying attention to were not so subtly sizing her up, as well.

When they reached the table, Logan pressed a kiss

to his mother's cheek, shook his father's hand and sent a wink in his sister's direction.

"Hey, everyone, I have someone I'd like you to meet." His hand was on Mallory's lower back, the pressure firm and reassuring. "This is Mallory Stevens. Mallory, these are my parents, Douglas and Melinda Bartholomew, and my kid sister, Laurel."

"Kid." Laurel sniffed. "I'm thirty-two. As Mom likes to point out, my biological clock is ticking like a time bomb with each passing day."

Logan shrugged. "Until you graduate from college with an actual degree, move out of Mom and Dad's house, and get a paying job, I'll consider you a kid."

"It's nice to meet you, Mallory." The young woman shook her hand before tagging on, "Even if I do question your taste in men."

"Laurel," their mother said evenly before turning her gaze on Mallory. Though the woman's smile was benign Mallory still felt as if she'd just wound up in a sniper's crosshairs. And for good reason, she decided, when Melinda said, "We didn't realize our son was seeing anyone until his brother called us this afternoon and mentioned that Logan and his girlfriend were coming by the restaurant."

Girlfriend. The moniker popped around in Mallory's head with the surprising effervescence of champagne bubbles. She wanted to turn and try to gauge Logan's reaction. Perhaps it would offer a key to how he was going to feel when she told him about the baby. But she didn't dare. Not with this attentive audience.

"She's not going to want to see me again if you guys don't stop interrogating her," he groused good-naturedly.

"We're not interrogating her. Yet," his father added in a comically ominous tone. Douglas patted the empty chair next to his. "Have a seat next to me, Mallory."

"I tried to warn you," she heard Logan mumble before he sat in a chair between his mother and sister.

Mallory found his family…interesting.

Half an hour in their company and she still couldn't quite figure them out. Usually she was good at sizing people up, but like Logan, the rest of the Bartholomew clan didn't fit into any of her preconceived notions. For instance, they were wealthy, but they didn't flaunt their status. Passing them on the street one wouldn't guess they ranked among the country's richest families.

Melinda's fingers sported only two rings, a tasteful gold wedding band on her left hand and what Mallory assumed to be a mother's ring, given its trio of birthstone gems, on the right one. Melinda was a lovely woman, but not an overly vain one. Her dark hair was streaked with silver in the front and the fine lines around her eyes crinkled into deeper creases when she smiled or laughed. No Botox for her.

Douglas's hair was a mix of dark blond and gray. It had a natural curl like his son's, though he wore it shorter and tamer. His build wasn't as athletic as Logan's, but he was hardly out of shape. Indeed, even though he had to be in his late sixties he could turn female heads. But it was clear, touchingly so, that he only had eyes for Melinda, his wife of forty years.

Like his father and older brother, Luke was a head turner. He stood taller than Logan and had a stockier build. His smile was easy and engaging. He'd popped out of the kitchen not long after their arrival and apologized for keeping them all waiting. The crowd was heavier than he'd anticipated and they were short a waitress. It would be a while yet before he could join them. He'd brought out more wine and a tray of appetizers. Mallory wondered if Logan noticed she hadn't touched the glass he'd poured for her earlier. Before returning to the kitchen, Luke had grinned at Mallory and bobbed his eyebrows in Logan's direction.

As for Laurel, she was a bit of a wild card. She had inherited her mother's dark hair and cheekbones, her father's long limbs and height, but none of their tact. She eyed Mallory with outright curiosity and just enough skepticism to make Mallory choose her words carefully whenever she spoke.

Even so, she was enjoying herself. Logan's family helped to explain a lot about him—his easy smile, for instance, and self-confident nature. Both came from a lifetime of his parents' love and support. Since he was a psychiatrist, she figured he understood the effect those things had on a person, but she wondered if he was as grateful for his good fortune as she found herself envious of it. Even now, her mother's love remained tainted by the bitterness of having to raise her daughter alone. As for support, Mallory's happiness and self-fulfillment came a distant second to her mother's desire to ensure her daughter was independent and self-sufficient.

"So, what do you do for a living?" Melinda asked. "Do you work at the radio station, too?"

"No. I'm a reporter with the *Herald*."

"A reporter." Douglas's eyebrows rose and he whistled through his teeth.

"At the *Herald*, you said?" This from Laurel. Something in her eyes put Mallory on guard.

"That's right," she said slowly.

"You cover city hall," his sister said.

"I did."

"She works in the Lifestyles section now," Logan inserted. "That's actually how we met. Mallory interviewed me for an advance on a speech I was giving."

"News reporting seems like such an exciting career," Melinda said. "I'd imagine you've met a lot of interesting people through your work."

"I have," she agreed.

"Me, for instance," Logan added, inducing a round of laughter that helped dilute Mallory's edginess.

It was back at full strength when Laurel said, "It seems an odd change of pace for someone to go from covering city politics to writing up lightweight feature stories."

"Laurel." Melinda's tone was disapproving. "You're being rude."

The younger woman shrugged. "I'm not trying to be. I just find it strange." Her gaze connected with Mallory's. "What prompted you to ask to be reassigned? If you don't mind my asking, that is," she added, presumably to appease her mother, who was glaring daggers at her. As for Logan, he looked as though he could have cheerfully wrung his sister's neck.

Mallory didn't care to be put in the hot seat, though she admired Laurel's go-for-the-throat technique. Bluntness was best met with honesty. Evasiveness would only raise more questions.

"Features, as you rightly note, are not my forte." She glanced at Logan then. "Although I have to admit that writing some of them has proven to be unexpectedly rewarding."

He smiled and that gave her courage. "The truth is I didn't ask to be reassigned from my city hall beat. I was removed from it. I screwed up." Admitting so in front of Logan wasn't as embarrassing as Mallory had thought it would be, perhaps because her job was no longer the epicenter of her life.

"There was a lawsuit," Laurel murmured, though her tone said she couldn't put a finger on the details.

Mallory decided to offer them now. "Yes. A big one that cost the newspaper a bundle in an out-of-court settlement. And it was my fault. I received information about suspected corruption from someone I considered a reliable source. I ran with it, even though I should have cross-checked the facts with other sources. I even used a quote from the mayor that came secondhand through one of his aides."

She'd been so eager to be the first to break the news, especially when her source claimed that reporters from other news agencies were sniffing around. She'd been a fool to believe him and then hung out to dry when he claimed under oath during a deposition that he'd never said the things Mallory claimed.

She had no tape recordings of their conversation, only hastily scribbled notes. It was her word against his, and though her editor would have supported her on that score, the lack of other sources and her insistence that they rush to print had sealed her fate.

"I let ambition cloud my judgment," she finished.

"That happens to us all from time to time," Douglas allowed with a sympathetic nod.

Melinda was more direct. "You've obviously paid for your mistake."

Mallory laughed without humor. "My editor doesn't see it that way yet. But then, I guess I can't really blame him since he got taken out to the woodshed along with me."

Barry Daniels had been allowed to keep his editorship, but per the terms of the settlement, the *Herald* was required to print a front-page apology and retraction. It didn't get much worse than that for a journalist.

"He must not be too angry with you. You still have a job," Laurel pointed out. The look on the young woman's face said she regretted opening this particular can of worms.

Oddly, Mallory was almost glad Laurel had. She glanced at Logan. In addition to telling him about the baby, there were other things that needed to be said, confessions to be made. Now was neither the time nor the place, but she felt compelled to admit, "I've been trying to get back into his good graces, remind him of my abilities by producing a killer story, but it's hard to come up with anything worthy of page one when my assignments aren't even as meaty as the stuff I wrote as a freshman for my college newspaper."

"I don't know. I seem to recall a riveting piece you penned on that speech I gave last month," he teased.

His mother smiled indulgently. "I clipped it out of the paper after reading it."

"Yeah, and it's still on the refrigerator," Laurel inserted with a roll of her eyes.

"So is the letter announcing that you made the dean's list last semester," Melinda reminded her. "As well as the starred review a food critic did of Luke's portabella mushroom burger." To Mallory she confided, "I don't believe in playing favorites. I'm proud of all of them."

Of course she was. They might be adults, but each was successful in his or her own way. And each could count on Melinda and Douglas's unending support. Lucky, Mallory thought again. So damned lucky. Her last call with her mother had been punctuated with nagging and complaining.

"You should write more stories about Logan," Laurel said. "People, and by people I mean women, love to read about him. He *is* the city's sexiest bachelor or some such nonsense."

Mallory's gaze connected with his across the table. He was smiling. The mood around the table was no longer tense. But she hoped he understood that she meant it when she said, "I'm going to leave stories about your brother to someone else to write."

* * *

It was just after midnight when Mallory and Logan left the Berkley Grill. Technically the restaurant closed at eleven, but even after the customers had gone and the wait staff had called it a night, the Bartholomews had stayed, sipping wine and coffee and sampling food. Mallory had stuck with water and avoided anything too spicy.

She was impressed with the fare and utterly awed by the affection she'd witnessed. With her deadbeat dad and bitter mom, she'd forgotten families could be like this: warm and close. Would her baby be so lucky?

"Your folks are really great," she told Logan as they walked hand in hand to his car. "And the rest of your family."

"You'll get no arguments from me. I even like my kid sister most of the time."

"Come on, you love her."

He shrugged. "That goes without saying. We're family."

"No, it doesn't go without saying," Mallory objected, thinking of her father. "Love isn't automatic just because you're related to someone."

"You're right. It's not."

"Half a dozen times tonight, I found myself thinking how lucky you are. I hope you know it."

"I do. I'm sorry about your dad, Mallory. Sorry not only for what he missed when you were young, but what he's missing out on now." They had arrived at his car and now stood at the passenger door. Instead of reaching for the handle, Logan reached for her. "You're an amazing woman," he whispered into her hair.

If she hadn't already known she was in love with him, she would have figured it out then and there. She still wasn't sure what to do about her emotions or where their relationship was heading, but she knew one thing for certain. She and Logan needed to talk.

CHAPTER TEN

LOGAN sat pitched forward on Mallory's couch, his right foot tapping on the polished hardwood floor as he waited for her to return from the kitchen, where she was getting them both a beverage.

Something was up.

He'd gotten that feeling on and off all evening. He might have attributed it to meeting his family or the awkwardness of his sister's questioning, but Mallory had been acting odd even before they arrived at the restaurant. And then on the way home she'd uttered the words that no man wanted to hear: "There's something I need to tell you."

He'd narrowed her bombshell—and he didn't doubt what she was gearing up to tell him was going to rock him back on his heels—to one of two things. She was either preparing to tell him she didn't want to see him anymore or she was going to tell him she was falling in love with him.

Logically, neither was a stretch. She'd met his entire family tonight. Things were getting serious between the two of them, which might just scare Mallory enough to make her cut and run. Or it might just give her the courage to declare the depth of her feelings for him.

Either possibility had his mouth going dry.

Logan didn't want to lose Mallory. He might not be ready for what was happening between them, but he wasn't a fool. These past couple of months with her had been nothing short of incredible. She had reawakened in him feelings he'd denied for a long time. But love? It was a big word that tended to lead to an even bigger commitment, one he wasn't sure he ever wanted to make again.

"Here's your wine," she said, smiling nervously when she returned. He noticed that she'd stuck with water. Keeping a clear head?

She handed him his glass and set hers on the end table. Before sitting next to him on the couch, she slipped off her shoes and tucked her bare feet up under herself. Even so she looked anything but relaxed.

He sipped his wine and waited. It was a moment before she broke the silence. When she did, it was with the benign comment: "I really enjoyed myself tonight."

"Good. I'm glad. I did, too."

"Do you get guys together often? As a family, I mean?"

Even as he wondered where the conversation was heading, he nodded. "Not as often as my mom would like since we're pretty busy these days. But we aim for Sunday dinner at my folks' house at least once a month."

"Who does the cooking?" She cocked her head to one

side and her expression verged on wistful. It was a sight to behold considering mere weeks ago *jaded* was an adjective his agent had used to describe Mallory.

"My mom, although she puts us all to work in the kitchen when she needs help."

"Even your dad?"

"Especially my dad." He laughed.

"That's nice." She smiled and reached for her water. "I have a confession to make." Uh-oh. Here we go. "I thought that since your folks are well-to-do they would have live-in help."

Okay, that wasn't exactly the confession Logan was expecting Mallory to make. He relaxed a little. Thinking about his family tended to have that effect. "When I was a kid we had a housekeeper who came in once a week, but generally speaking my mom prefers to do the cooking and what she calls 'homemaking.'" This time his smile was wistful. "My mom is proof there's a real art to keeping a nice and well-ordered home, raising children and arranging schedules to maximize together time."

"Did she ever work outside the home?"

He nodded. "She still does, after she retired from an accounting job she started volunteering at the Clearwater Project."

"I've heard of that. It promotes environmental responsibility, right?"

"Yes. My mom's new favorite color is green." Because their conversation was taking on the characteristics of an interview, he decided to ask some questions of his own. "What about your mom? What does she do?"

Mallory's expression was no longer wistful. "Well, she was the quintessential stay-at-home mother before the divorce. She used to bake cakes from scratch. She was a regular Martha Stewart but without the entrepreneurial flair. She was pretty meticulous about the house being clean, things being orderly.

"I used to think that was why my dad worked late so often. He didn't want to be nagged about where he'd taken off his shoes or how he'd forgotten to hang up his clothes." She shook her head and he wondered if she knew how sad she looked when she added, "It turned out he was spending his evenings with someone who didn't care in the least that he left his clothes on the bedroom floor."

"Sorry." He'd said that already once tonight in reference to her father.

She shook her head now. "I understand why my dad stepped out. It was wrong and I'm not making any excuses for his behavior, but I understand. What I don't understand is that my mom knew and she put up with it. Ultimately, he was the one who had to file for divorce."

"It sounds like financially it made sense for her to stay in the relationship, even though it wasn't a good one."

"I know, but—" Mallory shrugged "—my last boyfriend cheated on me. It was over as soon as I found out. I didn't wait for explanations. I didn't want any."

"Actions speak louder than words," he agreed.

"I know about your fiancée."

Logan hadn't seen that coming. Was this what she wanted to talk about? His tone cautious, he asked, "What do you know?"

"That the two of you were engaged to be married a decade ago, and a fall wedding was planned. Felicia married someone else, though."

"Did my mom tell you that the one time I excused myself to go to the men's room?"

Mallory's expression turned sheepish. "No. I did some digging on my own. It was just after you'd invited me onboard your sailboat the first time."

Mere weeks ago and yet it seemed an eternity.

"I see," he said evenly, though his blood pressure began to rise and his heart to sink.

"No, I don't think you do."

"You wanted a story." This time his tone wasn't even. It was crisp with anger—directed at her, but mostly at himself. How many times had his agent warned him that's what Mallory was after? Yet he'd trod boldly ahead. At first he'd claimed he knew what he was doing: keeping enemies closer than friends and all that baloney. Then, as things between Mallory and him had shifted, deepened, he'd insisted to himself that she wouldn't use him, she wouldn't betray him.

Well, he was paying for his hubris now. He sighed inwardly, felt the knife of disappointment pierce him. Had he really thought he could separate the woman from her profession? Especially knowing how important her job was to her.

He didn't really care that his broken engagement could become public knowledge. Let all of Chicago read about it and snicker over how he'd been played for a fool. What bothered him now was the fact that Mallory had dated him, slept with him, claimed the things he told her were off the record when apparently she'd considered him a story all along.

"Logan—"

He swore richly, cutting off her words. "Is that the best you could do?" he demanded. "You mentioned tonight that you're trying to get out of the doghouse at the newspaper. I doubt this is the type of story that is going to help you much. My ex-fiancée tossed me over for another guy." He shrugged, even though at one point that fact had all but lanced his soul. "I'm hardly the first man to suffer a broken heart."

"I'm sorry."

Logan finished off his wine and set the glass aside before rising to his feet. "What did you do to find that out? Run my name through a data base or something?"

"Nothing that high-tech. I just had to weed through some old newspaper clippings."

He stuffed his hands in his trouser pockets, concealing clenched fists. His tone was mild when he said, "That sounds time consuming."

"It took a few days."

"What made you look in the first place?"

Mallory shrugged. "I don't know. You just seemed, well, too perfect to be single."

"That's an interesting comment."

"Interesting or not, it's true."

"So you couldn't resist," he replied.

"I—"

"Don't get me wrong. What man doesn't want to be irresistible? It's just I'd prefer to be considered such for different reasons. But then you are a *reporter*." He spat out the word. "So...what? You put two and two together when you didn't find a wedding announcement?"

"Yes." Mallory cleared her throat and clarified, "Well, not for you."

"Ah." Turning away, he pulled his hands from his pockets and shoved the hair back from his forehead. He'd never felt this angry or this exposed. His voice was deceptively calm when he said, "You found the announcement for Felicia and what's his name?"

"I'm sorry," she murmured again.

Logan wasn't sure if Mallory was apologizing for snooping into his past or for the heartache he'd experienced at the hands of his ex—a heartache that felt minor in comparison to what he was feeling right now. He couldn't believe that once again he'd fallen for a beautiful woman's lies.

He was older now, wiser. Or so he'd thought. In addition to feeling betrayed, he felt like an absolute idiot. Usually he was insightful, astute. He was a trained professional with a degree that had taken him years to earn. It didn't sit well to learn that he had a blind spot a mile wide where Mallory was concerned.

When she'd told him they needed to talk, Logan hadn't seen this particular revelation coming. He'd worried over endings or possible new beginnings when apparently all she'd wanted was a damned interview.

Well, he'd give her one.

"So, what now?" It took an effort to keep all of the bitterness from leaching into his tone. "What else do you need to know to turn this rather mundane piece you're working on into something juicy?"

"It's not a story."

"Not yet it isn't," he agreed calmly. "You've got to throw in the stuff about me questioning my current career path, and the information about my television show contract will spice things up, too."

"Both of those things were said off the record," she replied, looking bewildered.

"We didn't agree to that till the revelations had been made. I'm sure that's some sort of loophole in your favor."

"Logan—"

He glanced away, determined not to be swayed. "Do you need a quote from me?"

"No. No!" she shouted and rose to her feet. He gave her points for looking both sincere and outraged. "I'm not asking for a damned quote, Logan."

Far from feeling relieved when she shared this news, he braced for the worst. "Is that because you already have one? Have you been in touch with my agent?"

Nina was going to read him the riot act if Mallory had called her.

"No."

"Felicia or her family then?" That possibility had his gut clenching.

"I haven't spoken to Felicia."

"Well, sorry, but I can't help you there. She left town not long after she married and she never gave me a forwarding address. I have no idea where she lives these days, and I haven't been in touch with her family to ask." He raised his brows and waited a beat before adding, "For obvious reasons."

"Actually, I know where Felicia is."

Mallory's bold pronouncement cut through his sarcasm with the force and effectiveness of a machete blade. Afterward, he felt laid bare.

"You…you know where…where Felicia…. Of course you do." He laughed humorlessly as he collected himself and then shook a finger in her direction. "Pit bull. Right. How could I forget?"

Mallory winced. Once upon a time she had relished that description. Hell, she'd gone out of her way to foster it. But she was ashamed of it now. Just as she was haunted by the way Logan was looking at her, even though a hundred other people whom she'd interviewed for stories for the newspaper during her career had looked at her in the exact same way: with utter contempt.

In the past she hadn't cared in the least. What did their opinions of her matter? Some of them—for that matter, most of them—were only getting exactly what they deserved. Their dirty little secrets deserved to be exposed and the public was better off for it. Right now, though, nothing—and certainly not a story—was as important as making Logan understand. He had to believe her. He had to trust her.

He had to *forgive* her. If he couldn't or wouldn't, how was she going to tell him about the baby?

"I know where Felicia is, but I haven't contacted her."

"Yet."

"Don't, Logan. I've finally decided to stop selling myself short. Don't you start now." When so much was at stake. "I have no intention of calling Felicia for a quote or anything else."

He said nothing, but the rigid set of his shoulders told Mallory that he didn't quite believe her. She reached out a hand to him, but he was too far away to touch…physically as well as emotionally. The heart she'd worked so hard to gird from breaking suffered its first fissures and began to ache.

She pressed ahead. "Weren't you listening tonight at the restaurant when I told you that I wouldn't be writing any stories where you're concerned? I meant it."

"Why?" he asked.

"I think you know."

"Spell it out, Mallory." His tone was barely above a whisper as he made the command. "Be clear."

"There are a few reasons. One is that doing so would be a conflict of interest."

His brow wrinkled as he studied her, and he crossed his arms over his chest. "A conflict of interest? How so?"

"Isn't it obvious?"

"I said to be clear," he reminded her, though neither his tone nor his stance was quite as rigid as it had been just a moment earlier.

"I... I..." It was a big word for an even bigger emotion. She took a tentative step in his direction, gathering her courage when he didn't back away. "I love you, Logan."

He didn't say anything at first, but he blinked a couple of times and swallowed. She was pretty sure she'd thrown him with that revelation, and even though she wanted to hear him say it in return—God, how she wanted that—it wasn't fair to put him on the spot.

"I'm not expecting you to say anything right now. I just..." She clasped and unclasped her hands. "I just wanted you to know."

"Anything else you want me to know?"

I'm having your baby.

But she decided to keep that information confidential. Sharing it now, with this other big issue unresolved between them, would only complicate matters. Mallory shook her head.

"When I asked you to come with me tonight, I can honestly say I didn't think the evening would end this way," he said after a moment.

"No." Was he saying goodbye? Neither his expression nor his body language gave his intent away.

"I'm sorry, Mallory."

It wasn't exactly what she'd hoped to hear. Arms crossed over her waist as if to protect the life growing inside her from rejection, she braced for his farewell.

"It's all right." The words cost her.

"No. It's not." He closed the distance between them, lifted her chin with his finger. "I'm sorry for doubting you, for jumping to conclusions. Forgive me?"

He was asking for contrition?

"I don't understand. I thought…I thought you were going to say that things between us are over."

"I may be a fool, but I'm not that big a fool."

"I should have told you about the information I'd found. I didn't mean for it to be a secret. It's just that I gathered it before anything had really taken place between us and, well, afterward, when I decided you were more important to me than any story…"

"Because you love me." He looked pleased now.

"Yes."

"Well, I have a scoop for you, and I don't care who knows it." His hands found her hips and pulled her close. Just before he kissed her, he said, "I love you, too."

CHAPTER ELEVEN

THE next few weeks passed in a wondrous haze. Mallory couldn't recall ever being so happy or feeling so complete, which was odd considering she was still writing intern-worthy fluff for the *Herald*'s Lifestyles section and having to put up with Sandra's snide comments whenever their paths crossed at work. Lately Sandra wasn't only snide, she seemed smug. Mallory dismissed it. Her colleague was the last person on her mind.

Indeed, work in general continued to take a back seat. She spent less time at the office, putting in the standard number of hours and no more, unless specifically asked by the features editor. Where a few months earlier she would have spent most of her waking hours breathing in newsprint and combing through wire service stories, she now spent her evenings with Logan at her home or on his sailboat or in his upscale condominium, where he was attempting to teach her the rudiments of cooking in his gorgeous gourmet kitchen. She was learning a great deal, not only about sautéing, basting and frying, but about herself. As she'd told him that night in her apartment, she'd stopped selling herself short.

Mallory liked who she was when she was with Logan. She felt no need to be perfect or to cloak herself in a mantle of toughness. As flawed as she was, he enjoyed spending time with her. He said he loved her. Even so, she still hadn't told him about the baby, whose existence had now been confirmed by her doctor.

Though she told herself not to be, she was a little scared. What would his reaction be? She had to believe he would be happy and supportive despite their circumstances. And surely he would be the polar opposite of her father in every way. A lifetime of hurt, however, was not easy to overcome. Besides, she had time. She was barely two months along. And everything between her and Logan was so new, so perfect. She wanted to give them both time to adjust to being a couple before introducing the fact that they were to become parents.

Mallory was bustling around her apartment rounding up a change of clothes and trying to remember what she'd done with the white chef's apron she'd bought, when the telephone rang. She assumed it was Logan since they were eating in at his condo tonight. He was going to teach her how to make an authentic Chinese stir-fry.

She grinned as she picked up the receiver. "Be patient, lover," she said on a laugh.

"Mallory? Is that you?" On top of the usual agitation in her mother's voice, Maude sounded perplexed.

Mallory sorely regretted not consulting the Caller ID readout. Not only was this conversation bound to be a downer, it was guaranteed to be long.

"Yeah, Mom. Sorry about the greeting. I thought you were someone else."

"That much I gathered," Maude said dryly and with a touch of censure.

"I'm…I'm just on my way out the door, Mom. I have someplace I need to be and I'm already running a little behind. Can I call you back later?"

"By later I assume you mean tomorrow." Not a touch of censure now, but a slap of it, and that was before Maude added, "I thought you'd sworn off men after the last one. What was his name?"

Mallory didn't bother to supply it. The past was irrelevant. "I've met someone special, Mom."

"Oh, no." It wasn't exactly what a woman wanted to hear from her mother in response to a statement like that. "You sound like you think you're in love."

"I don't think it." Mallory left it at that, already regretting mentioning her relationship with Logan. Thank God her mother was clueless about the baby.

"Don't fall into the same trap I did," Maude warned before launching into her old rant. "I wasted fourteen years of my life waiting on your father, making a home for him and putting his needs ahead of my own. You know what I had to show for it when he left me? Nothing."

You had me, Mallory wanted to say. You had a daughter who felt deserted by not one but two parents.

But she knew the futility of trying to rationalize or argue. Maude wanted sympathy and agreement. Mallory couldn't bring herself to offer either, so she substituted them with silence.

Her mother seemed not to notice. "You make a good living at the newspaper," she went on. "You have a career, money, a purpose, all of the things I should have had and would have had in my twenties if I hadn't let your father talk me into marriage and letting him provide for me. I thought I was in love back then, too."

Again Mallory had to bite her tongue, since if her parents had never met she wouldn't have been born. Her mother's bitterness had blinded her to how insulting and hurtful her comments could be.

"You have a good life, Mallory. I'll be very disappointed in you if you let some man ruin it," Maude finished.

This wasn't a new tack her mother took. She'd been saying much the same thing since Mallory's first date at age fifteen. For the first time, though, instead of rolling her eyes and letting it pass without remark, Mallory got angry. Angry enough to break her cardinal rule and argue.

"A good life, Mom? Is that what you think I have?" Until recently, it had been so pathetically empty, so work focused and one dimensional. Spending time with Logan, falling in love with him, made her see that clearly. "Just because I'm single doesn't mean my life has been good."

The rebuttal—the words as much as their crisp

delivery—must have thrown Maude. Mallory pictured her mother's mouth working soundlessly on the other end of the line. It was a wonderful moment, an amazingly liberating one, especially since Mallory hadn't even realized she'd been as tethered to the past as her mother.

But all good things must come to an end, and her mother's silence was one of them.

"That's the way you talk to me? After all of the sacrifices I've made through the years to see to it that you could have everything I didn't and couldn't?"

Mallory almost apologized, not because she felt contrite, but because she could wind up the conversation that much more quickly if she gave in, gave up. A glance at her watch showed that she was already going to be late arriving at Logan's condo. Well, whether a little late or a lot, this couldn't wait. For once, she was going to set the record straight.

"I appreciate your sacrifices, Mom. I always have. What I don't appreciate is the way you've used them as a battering ram, trying to ensure I would always feel beholden to you. You did what a parent is expected to do and, okay, more since Dad skipped out on his obligations after he left."

"After he left!" Maude spat the words. "He wasn't much of a father while he was still in the home. You have no idea the sacrifices I made," she said a second time.

Mallory decided to try a different approach. "You could have more now, Mom. You could go back to school, take some courses so you could get a job you actually liked."

Maude snorted. "At my age?"

"You're fifty-four. That's hardly ancient."

"He's really turned your head, hasn't he? This fellow you're rushing off to see." Her mother sounded disgusted.

"He's a good man." The very best. And he was going to be a good father. She would believe that. She wouldn't let the past poison the future.

"They all start off that way."

"No. They don't." The truth struck Mallory with enough force that she leaned against the kitchen wall for support. "None of the guys I dated in the past started off treating me very well. Maybe that's what I wanted," she murmured, half to herself. "Maybe, after what happened between you and Dad, I didn't want to be tempted to have a serious relationship, one with long-term possibilities."

She was tempted now. More than tempted, she decided. And the baby growing inside her wasn't the only reason.

"Mallory—"

Her mother was gearing up for another depressing diatribe, but Mallory had heard enough. Nothing she'd said to Maude had changed her mother's mind, but at least Mallory had had her say and experienced an epiphany of her own.

"Mom. I've got to go. Logan is waiting for me."

* * *

"You look different," Logan said as she stood chopping a red bell pepper at the kitchen counter.

She was using the Santoku knife the way he'd taught her, keeping the tip of the blade on the cutting board and levering the rest of it up and down to cut the vegetable. She'd already given the same treatment to an onion and a couple stalks of celery for the shrimp stir fry they were making.

"It's your fancy lighting." She used the knife to point to the trio of amber-glass pendant lights that hung above the counter, but a panicky part of her wondered if he could tell she was pregnant just by looking at her.

"No." His eyes narrowed speculatively. "It's more than that."

"You're making me feel self-conscious," she warned when he continued to stare at her. "I'm liable to slice off a finger if you keep inspecting me like that."

He wasn't deterred by the prospect of bloodshed. "You look...lighter."

Mallory blinked at that before setting the knife aside and crossing her arms over her chest. "Are you saying you thought I was fat before?"

He chuckled. "Not lighter in that regard. Lighter in spirit I guess is what I mean."

She made a tsking noise. "Watch it. You're coming awfully close to analyzing me."

"Not close. I am." He plucked a piece of red pepper from the cutting board and popped it in his mouth. "So, what's happened?"

Where to begin, Mallory thought. She unfolded her

arms and decided to keep to the most recent event. "I talked to my mother just before coming here."

"Oh." He nodded. "Is that why you were late?"

"Yes." She wiped her hands on the front of her white chef's apron, not because they were dirty, but because her palms suddenly felt moist.

"Is she okay?"

"Yes." Then Mallory shook her head. "No, not really. I feel sorry for her."

"How so?"

Logan was all doctor now, but Mallory didn't mind. She'd come to appreciate this side of him. His calm assessments and keen insights. She offered some of her own. "My dad did a real number on her, but it was years ago."

"Sometimes the passage of time is irrelevant if the hurt was substantial enough." When she frowned, he said quietly, "I let ten years pass before I found myself in another serious relationship."

"Because of Felicia."

He nodded and the revelation caused Mallory to swallow. They had talked about a lot of things since that night in her apartment, but by unspoken agreement, they'd steered clear of this topic.

"A little ironic, huh?" His expression turned sardonic. "I counsel people on relationships, on moving forward with their lives despite adversity or after heartache. Yet I spent the better part of a decade in emotional limbo."

"You're not in limbo now." She rose on tiptoe and kissed him.

"Nope." He nipped at her lower lip.

"You've moved on with your life."

"Full steam ahead," he agreed. Then he sobered. "You know, I'm still not sure if I prefer what I'm doing to being in private practice, but for the first time since I went on the air, I no longer feel like a fraud."

"I'm glad."

"So, what happened with your mom?"

"She needs to move on. Forget limbo. The woman is in purgatory and she's only too happy to try to drag me there, too. She's lonely and bitter and absolutely determined to remain that way."

"Have you accepted that her unhappiness is not your fault or your responsibility?"

"Oh, I accepted that a long time ago. What occurred to me today when she began lecturing me on the evils of men and relationships—" when Logan's brows lifted, Mallory inserted "—yes, my mother finds your species to be without redemption. Anyway, when she trotted out the same old saw today, I got so angry that I actually argued with her."

"You've never argued with your mother before? You?" he said again, his lips beginning to twitch.

"Are you insinuating that I'm contrary?"

He leaned forward to drop a kiss on the tip of her nose. "I wouldn't dare. Now, go on with your story."

"I've argued with my mom about plenty of things,

but not about men in general or my dad in particular. I've always just let her have her say," Mallory admitted.

"Avoidance," he murmured.

"Maybe. Probably." She shrugged. "But I didn't think I'd put any stock in her words or that they'd had any impact on my life. Until today."

"What changed?" he asked softly and reached for her hand. His fingers weaved through hers, a symbol of the bond that had formed between them. It gave her strength and Mallory smiled.

"I changed. I realized that until recently I was a workaholic. I didn't just enjoy my job, I'd made it the focus of my life to the exclusion of all else. Well, except for loser guys."

"Present company excluded, I hope."

"Definitely. The men I dated in the past were…so wrong for me. I knew that, on a subconscious level at least, but I didn't want to get serious with anyone. I didn't want to chance a repeat of my mother's life." She shook her head slowly. "The funny thing is I was already living her life. Sure, the circumstances were different—no jerky ex-husband, no child to raise without support." Her heart thudded at that, but she pressed on. "No mediocre job to toil away at because I didn't have a college degree or marketable skills—but I had become every bit as lonely and jaded."

"Wow." He nodded appreciatively. "No wonder you look so light. You shed a ton of baggage."

"Yeah." She smiled. "I did." They both had.

"And you did it all by yourself." He pretended to

frown. "You know, if more people could do what you just did, I'd be out of a job."

"But I'd still need you, Logan." She raised their linked hands to kiss the back of his. "Thank you."

Logan's smile was gentle, his steady gaze mesmerizing. "For what?"

"For not being a jerk."

He laughed. "Thanks, I think."

"I'm starving." She released his hand, but instead of going back to chopping vegetables, Mallory began to untie the apron strings.

"What are you doing?"

Instead of answering his question, she asked one of her own. "Ever made love in a kitchen?"

"This kitchen?" His voice was hoarse and his gaze darkened when she tossed the apron aside and started undoing the buttons on her blouse.

"Or any kitchen."

"No."

"Neither have I." Her blouse joined the apron on the floor. Her bra was new, a sleek and sexy number that created cleavage with the aid of an underwire. Her stomach was still flat, but her breasts were a little fuller, so she looked good wearing it as well as the matching pair of panties that were under her skirt. She unhooked her cotton skirt and let it slide down her legs. If she'd had doubts about her appearance, one look at Logan's expression would have dispelled them.

"Ask me again in an hour." He tugged the tails of his shirt free from his blue jeans and began to unfasten the buttons. She caught a glimpse of his muscular chest and the hair that covered it.

"An hour, huh? That's a long time. You must be feeling pretty confident."

Logan moaned. "I'm feeling a lot of things."

While she was nearly naked, he was mostly clothed.

Mallory appreciated the fact that Logan liked to take his time when it came to intimacy, but his progress with his shirt was much too slow for liking. She nudged his hands aside and made fast work of the remaining buttons.

Need was building, arcing dangerously between them like the current from an exposed wire.

"A lot can happen in an hour," he said as she pushed the shirt off his broad shoulders.

"That's what I'm counting on."

"A reporter from the *Herald* is on the telephone. She insists on speaking to you," Logan's secretary informed him just after he wrapped up his morning show. "Should I take a message?"

"No." He smiled, recalling the scene in his kitchen a couple evenings earlier. And the scene in his bedroom later that same night. And the scene in the shower the following morning. If they kept this up they were liable to kill each other. But what a way to go. "Put her through."

"I was just thinking of you," he said in lieu of a greeting.

"Really? That's a surprise."

And so was the voice on the other end of the line. It didn't belong to Mallory.

Logan straightened in his seat. "My apologies. I thought you were someone else," he replied stiffly.

"Obviously. I think I know exactly who you mean. I'm Sandra Hutchins. We met briefly at a charity dinner a couple months back."

"I remember. Why are you calling?"

"I'd like you to confirm some information for me," she began. "I recently learned that you were engaged to a Felicia Grant ten years ago."

Logan had a sick feeling, but he managed to keep wariness from his tone when he said, "Yes. So?"

"You didn't marry."

"No, we didn't."

"Why?" the woman had the audacity to ask.

"You know, I don't really see how that's your business, Miss Hutchins."

"Infidelity, I believe, was the culprit," she went on as if he hadn't spoken. "Miss Grant married another man mere months after your wedding was called off."

"Old news," he said nonchalantly.

"Perhaps." The gleeful note in her tone worried him. "I assume you understand perfectly the reason Miss Grant divorced her husband less than a year after their marriage?"

"I wasn't aware she'd divorced. She left town almost immediately after they got married, and I saw no reason to keep in touch with her family."

"Really? *No* reason?"

Something was off here. Way off. Mallory had dug up this very same information, but Sandra was acting as if she had a huge bombshell to drop. Logan couldn't imagine what it might be.

"I'm sorry to hear Felicia's marriage fell apart. Contrary to what you apparently think, I harbor no ill feelings for her, especially after all this time."

And especially now that he'd fallen in love with Mallory. The past was the past. It was the present and the future he wanted to concentrate on now.

"What about your son? What feelings, if any, do you harbor for him?"

CHAPTER TWELVE

LOGAN couldn't breathe. He sucked air in through his mouth, but it didn't seem to make it all the way to his lungs.

"What are you talking about?" he managed after a lengthy pause during which he pictured Sandra smiling gleefully on the other end of the line.

"Little Devon Michael Getty. Well, he's not so little now. While Felicia's ex was kind enough to provide the boy with his surname, it's obvious you provided the DNA. He bears a striking resemblance to you, Dr. Bartholomew."

A child? A son? No. It wasn't true. It couldn't be. Could it?

While nothing made sense at the moment, one thing was clear: Logan was not going to continue talking to a reporter on the record, especially when he didn't know what he was talking about.

He gathered his scattered wits and managed to sound authoritative when he snapped, "This conversation is over."

Even before he cleared the radio station's lobby, he was on his cell phone with his agent. Briefly, he explained the situation, hoping Nina would offer some words of wisdom. Her response was anything but reassuring.

"I knew your getting mixed up with Mallory Stevens was a bad idea."

"This has nothing to do with Mallory."

"It's a different reporter who called you today, but from the same paper. Don't be naive, Logan. Mark my word, she had a hand in this. What have you said to her regarding your former fiancée?"

"Nothing. Well, very little. She admitted a while ago that she knew about Felicia and was aware of our breakup. She never explored it further. That was the end of it."

"*She* didn't," his agent stressed. "She handed it over to someone else."

Logan swore. No. He wouldn't believe that. "This isn't about Mallory. For that matter, it's not even about a damned news story."

"The one in question could very well cripple your career, not to mention cost you the nationally syndicated television show," Nina reminded him. "The contract has been signed, but the fine print clearly allows them to yank the plug under certain circumstances. I think this would qualify."

His agent was paid to think about business and his image, which is why he'd called her. Let her perform damage control. Logan had bigger issues to worry about. My God, what was Mallory going to think when she heard this news? Another thought struck like a blow. Had she already?

"Do whatever you think needs to be done, Nina. I'll be in touch later. I've got to get to the bottom of this," he said, hanging up even as his agent was still sputtering in outrage.

Did he have a son, a boy old enough to be just as confused and hurt by his defection as Mallory had been by her father's? He needed to find the truth. For that he had to talk to Felicia. Unfortunately, Logan didn't know where to find her.

But Mallory did.

Despite the rain, Logan stood on the deck of his sailboat, waiting for Mallory to arrive. After the cryptic phone call he'd left on her office voice mail, he would have understood if Mallory hadn't come. He must have sounded unbalanced, asking her to meet him, to bring her notes on Felicia, and not to tell anyone at her office where she was heading. He spied her jogging along the dock under the protection of a polka-dotted umbrella and sighed in relief.

Mallory didn't know what to make of Logan's desperate-sounding message or their clandestine meeting. But she never questioned going. They had tickets for a Sox game that evening, but he wouldn't have asked her to break away from work in the middle of the day to meet him on his sailboat without a good reason.

When she reached him, she noted that his hair was wet, his oxford shirt soaked through. Something was troubling him, though his manners were unaffected. He helped her aboard the *Tangled Sheets* and ushered her below deck.

"My God. You're drenched." Even so, she didn't protest when he pulled her against him. He needed her. That much was clear.

"Sorry," he mumbled as he pulled away. "Now you're drenched, too."

"Don't worry about me."

"Don't worry about you?" He cocked his head to one side. "I can't help worrying about you. It comes with the territory, you know." His expression was fierce when he said, "I love you, Mallory."

"I know. I love you, too."

"Remember you said that."

She frowned at the odd request. Some of the old doubts whispered in her head. The voice sounded suspiciously like that of her mother. Though the voice wouldn't be silenced, she refused to listen to it. "Logan, you're scaring me. Please, tell me why you asked me to meet you here."

"You haven't spoken to Sandra, then."

Her stomach heaved. It had been doing that ever since she'd retrieved his phone message. She wasn't sure if stress or pregnancy was the culprit.

"Sandra Hutchens? I go out of my way to avoid her. What does Sandra have to do with this?"

"There's something we need to discuss."

Mallory couldn't agree more. She'd already decided she wanted to confide in him about her pregnancy. She'd planned to do it tonight, after the ball game. It was time he knew. She was growing more excited by the day. She wanted him to share in it. Besides, he was an astute man, a doctor by training. He'd figure it out soon enough if she continued to avoid alcohol and munch on saltine crackers to calm her nausea. He'd have every right to be angry with her then.

"You brought your notes, right?"

"Yes." She reached into her satchel and pulled them out. Other than her editor, no one was privy to what was inside the small spiral notebook. She didn't hesitate, though, before asking Logan what he needed.

"Felicia's contact information."

Mallory must have stumbled back a step. The next thing she knew he was holding her by the arms. "You want Felicia's number?"

"I wouldn't ask if it wasn't important. Something's come up." He laughed harshly. "Actually, Sandra has brought something up. I need to find out if it's true."

"What...?" She let the words trail off and fought the urge to pepper him with questions. Now was not the time to turn on her reporter mode. Instead she ripped a piece of paper from her notebook and handed it to him. "Here."

"Just like that?"

She swallowed, nodded. "No questions asked."

He kissed her hard and quick. "I'll let you ask all of the questions you want…later. Right now I have to get to the bottom of some things. It might take a while."

She nodded, determined to stay strong. "That's all right. I've got to get back to the office, anyway. Can you meet me at my apartment this evening?"

"I'll come by right after I finish with my lawyer."

"Lawyer! Are you in some kind of trouble, Logan?" Without waiting for him to reply, she offered, "What can I do? What do you need?"

"I need you," he said quietly. "See you later?"

"I'll be waiting." *We'll both be waiting*, she added silently.

Mallory didn't get much work done after returning to the office. How could she? Briefly she'd considered contacting Logan's family. As close-knit as the Bartholomew clan was, surely his parents or one of his siblings would know what was going on. But she refrained. She could wait till this evening. Logan would explain the situation, and together they would figure out how to deal with whatever it was that was causing him so much distress.

She was staring at her blank computer screen when her phone rang. It was the editor.

"I need to see you in my office."

In the past being summoned to Barry's office hadn't filled Mallory with trepidation. Heck, she'd barged in without an invitation often enough when she was working on a good story. Today, between nerves and the baby, she felt downright nauseated, and her queasiness intensified when she spied Sandra sitting to one side of his desk.

"Shut the door," Barry told her.

Mallory had the odd feeling that her fate was being sealed as it closed.

"What's up?" she asked, striving for casual.

"Sandra is working on a story, one that will be an exclusive if we can wrap it up quickly."

"How very enterprising of you," Mallory remarked. "What does it have to do with me?"

"She's dug up some rather damning information on a local celebrity. The facts are pretty solid, but our lawyers are demanding we ensure every *i* is dotted and every *t* crossed. They've become a little gun-shy these days."

Mallory's heart had begun to pound so loudly that she had to strain her ears to hear what Sandra was saying. "Let's just cut to the chase, shall we? I need an interview with Logan Bartholomew and, given how chummy the two of you have become lately, I figure you can help me get it."

"Why do you need an interview with Logan?" But she knew. Felicia. It was all starting to make sense.

"You can read the answer to that in the paper when the story breaks."

Mallory stiffened her spine. "You think I'll help you?"

"We're all on the same team," the editor inserted.

"Sandra has offered to give you credit for contributing to her report in a tagline at the end the story."

Did they really think Mallory was holding out for credit? Perhaps the old Mallory would have. The one who put work above everything, including personal relationships.

"Sorry. I can't help you."

The response had Sandra cursing and the editor blowing out a breath. "Fine," Barry said after a moment. "I'll spring you from features."

It was what she'd wanted when she'd pursued Logan in the beginning. She couldn't help but think she was partly to blame for his current mess. Whatever juicy tidbit Sandra had managed to unearth, Mallory was the one who had started the digging.

Ignoring the editor's offer, she turned to her rival. "I have to hand it to you, Hutchens. You're brighter than you look. You saw me riffling through the files that night in the morgue and actually put two and two together."

"I hope you're not going to accuse me of poaching your story." Glancing at the editor, Sandra said, "I merely picked up where she left off, since it didn't appear she was going to do anything with the information."

"I made it pretty easy, even for someone with your poor instincts," Mallory snapped.

Sandra ignored the insult. "You signed out all those clip files in my name and then took your sweet time turning them in." Her smile was both malicious and triumphant. "It made me wonder just what you were up to. Then I saw you with Logan and remembered seeing you reading his engagement announcement."

Mallory was the one who swore this time. "Well, I can't help you out any further."

"Can't or won't?" Sandra asked. "I need to speak to him."

"Sorry." She lifted her shoulders.

Sandra turned to the editor. "I want an exclusive! For the paper, of course."

"Of course," Mallory muttered. Had she really been as driven as Sandra? As blind to everything and everyone around her?

"The lawyers want us to include a response from either Bartholomew or someone authorized to speak on his behalf," the editor said. "Sorry, Sandra. I'm not willing to stick my neck out again." His gaze slid to Mallory before he added, "It still has ax marks on it from the last time."

A moment ago Mallory had been offered a way out of the doghouse, but Barry was letting her know that unless she helped them, she would remain in it.

Sandra stood, braced her hands on his desk and leaned forward. The pose was menacing, but her voice verged on whining when she said, "But, Barry, we can't wait much longer. If we do, one of the other news outlets is bound to scoop us. It's just a matter of time as it is till the news breaks, especially since Venture Media has offered Bartholomew a syndicated television show."

So, they knew about that, too. Mallory tried to

downplay the situation. "What's the big deal? So the guy was dumped by his ex and then had a hard time trusting women. He may be a psychiatrist, but he's also human."

Sandra turned, her eyes lighting up with almost maniacal delight. "He hasn't told you. My God, you, journalist extraordinaire Mallory Stevens, are in the dark." She clapped her hands together. "I love it! I absolutely love it!"

"Sandra," Barry began, looking uncharacteristically uncomfortable as he divided a look between the two women.

Sandra ignored him. "Please, Barry. At least let me break *this* story."

"What are you talking about?" Mallory demanded through clenched teeth.

"Your darling doctor is a daddy. The deadbeat variety."

If she hadn't been sitting, Mallory's legs would have buckled. "What?"

"You heard me. Logan has a son. A nine-year-old boy he fathered with Felicia, and I have it on good authority that he's never seen or so much as tried to contact the kid, much less paid any child support."

Mallory shook her head, unconsciously covering her abdomen with one shaking hand. "You're wrong. Logan doesn't…and even if he did he wouldn't… You're mistaken."

"No. I'm not. Unless the birth certificate is wrong.

You're not only a sloppy reporter, Mallory, you're a damned fool."

Sandra sailed out of Barry's office then, leaving Mallory shell-shocked and reeling. Her humiliation was complete when her stomach heaved and she was forced to wretch in the editor's wastepaper basket.

Barry offered the box of tissue rather than any sympathy.

"I won't even ask about half the stuff Sandra just said, all I want to know is if you're going to help."

She wiped her lips, would have killed for a breath mint. She settled for a stiff spine. "No. I thought I'd already made that clear."

"Come on," he cajoled. "We both know you did half the legwork on this story. Help Sandra finish it and you can get back to doing what you do best."

Hard news. Real stories. Meaty pieces about scandals, lawbreaking and deceit. She was a journalist. She would always enjoy breaking news. But she wouldn't exploit her relationship with Logan to do it, especially since she didn't consider this to be on par with government bribes, police cover-ups or accounting irregularities at city hall. If what Sandra claimed was true, it was Logan's private hell, and she had to believe he had an explanation. He wasn't a deadbeat. He wasn't anything like her father. He'd given her nothing but reasons to trust him. She wouldn't start doubting him now when he needed her most.

"No," she told Barry.

When Mallory rose to her feet, he asked, "Where do you think you're going?"

To tell the father of my unborn child how much I love him. To help him through his current crisis. She wasn't going to walk away from him now, and she certainly wasn't going to play an active role in the effort to destroy his life.

"Mallory," Barry shouted when she reached his door. "I asked where you're going."

"Home. I don't feel well." But she knew what to do to make herself better.

It was nine-twenty when Logan knocked at Mallory's door. Logan was wiped out emotionally and physically, his adrenaline used up. He'd contacted Felicia and spent a couple of hours on the phone with her, and later with her parents. It made him feel marginally better that they hadn't known Devon's true paternity. Like everyone else, they had assumed that Nigel Getty was the child's father. Apparently only Nigel and Felicia had known the whole truth. That she'd discovered her pregnancy after breaking off her engagement to Logan.

Nigel and Felicia had gone ahead with their wedding, both hoping the child would turn out to be Nigel's. But almost immediately after Devon's birth it became apparent he favored Logan. Their marriage had lasted a year. Ironically, while Nigel had had no problem becoming involved with an engaged woman, the idea of raising a son he had not fathered had proven beyond his ability. When a paternity test confirmed that Devon was

Logan's, Nigel filed for divorce. At his insistence, the birth certificate was changed to reflect the boy's true parentage. But neither Logan nor Devon was ever told the truth.

Logan was angry, bitter. He felt betrayed all over again by Felicia, but it was worse this time. He was a father. He had a son. And they were absolute strangers.

Weighing almost as heavily on his mind was what Mallory's reaction was going to be to the news. Would she believe him? Would she accept that he'd had no idea of Felicia's pregnancy when they'd parted ways? Or would she view the situation through the filter of her past and come to the same assumption Sandra had: that he'd happily walked away from his responsibility.

Just as Mallory's father had all those years ago.

Logan tried to smile when the door opened. Mallory's face was ashen, but her shoulders were squared. Something in her expression told him she already knew what he was going to tell her. More than anything he wanted to hold her. He needed her understanding as much as he needed her comfort and support. But he held back, waiting for some sign that she would offer them.

"I was getting worried," she said.

"Sorry. It took a little longer than I'd anticipated."

After his conversations with Felicia and her family, he'd spent time with his lawyer. There would not be a custody battle. Logan and his son were strangers. It would be cruel and traumatic to try to wrench the boy away from Felicia, even though Logan had every intention of being an involved father. A visitation schedule would be worked out as well as financial support.

"Come in," she said.

Stepping into the well-lit foyer, he could see that Mallory was pale and looked drawn. "You look like I feel. Everything okay?"

"The editor summoned me to his office after I returned to the newspaper."

His heart sank. "I think I can guess why."

"Sandra was quite gleeful about the whole matter."

"Yeah, I got that feeling when she reached me at the station the other day and dropped the bomb." He wondered if the shrapnel wounds would ever heal. "Mallory, about the boy—"

"You didn't know."

Her tone held absolutely no equivocation. And here Logan had thought he couldn't love her more than he already did. Given her past, Mallory had every reason not to believe him. But she did. She did.

"Thank you for that. I was worried that you'd think—"

She stopped his words with a kiss. "No. I'm done living in the past, remember? They want a quote from you, by the way, and they want me to get it." She tilted her head to one side. "Sandra said she'd give me a bit of credit in the story tagline. The editor was more generous than that. He offered to spring me from the Lifestyles section."

"If I have to talk to someone, I'd rather it be you. And if you get your old beat back in the process that will make it worthwhile."

Mallory frowned. "You think I agreed to do it? I just told you I'm done living in the past. My job is no longer my life, Logan. I won't use you to get back into the newsroom. It's not worth it."

"I wouldn't mind."

"I would. I love you."

"I love you right back." He kissed her and Mallory smiled.

"See, no job can do that."

As relieved as he was at the moment, Logan was also a realist. They had more to discuss, more decisions to make. He led her to the couch and pulled her down next to him.

"My life is about to become a three-ring circus," he began. "My agent informed me on the way here that the contract for my syndicated show has been nullified."

"Sorry."

"I thought I would be, too. But I'm not. It wasn't the direction I wanted to go professionally. They'll be releasing a statement to the media since the rumors of a deal were already circulating. It's going to get really complicated."

"Are you trying to give me an out?"

"Just for a little while. I don't want you to get struck by any of the mud that's about to get flung."

"That's sweet, but I'm not going anywhere. We're in this together, Logan."

"I was hoping that was what you'd say. I need you, Mallory." He shoved a hand through his hair, his composure crumpling. "My God, I have a son. A son. He's nine years old and he doesn't know who I am, and I don't know the first thing about him or, for that matter, about being a father."

"You'll be a great dad."

He appreciated her conviction, but his voice caught when he said, "I've missed so much stuff that I shouldn't have missed. Forget walking and talking, he's already riding a bike, playing baseball. I can't believe Felicia kept this from me all these years."

Logan's pain was plainly visible. Mallory's heart ached for him. "I'm so sorry."

"Felicia and I talked for a long time. I can't believe she did what she did, especially keeping Devon from me even after she knew the truth. But what's done is done. Arguing about it now won't solve anything."

"So what will you do?"

"Felicia was already considering returning to Chicago. Her business in Portland is failing, and now that I know about Devon she doesn't really have any reason to remain there. After I meet Devon and get to know him well enough that he's comfortable spending time alone with me, we're going to work out a visitation arrangement. So part of the time it won't be just the two of us."

Mallory had planned to tell Logan about their child tonight, and part of her still wanted to, but it wouldn't be fair. He had so much on his plate right now. Her news would keep. For another day or a couple weeks at most. Just until Logan caught his second wind.

* * *

Two weeks passed. Not surprisingly, the media, both in Chicago and nationally, had a field day as the story of Logan's nine-year-old "love child" leaked out.

The tabloids and some Internet blogs questioned Logan's claims that he hadn't known about his son, despite Felicia's statements supporting that version of events. Mallory could only imagine what would be written if anyone was privy to news of her pregnancy. She was still keeping it under wraps. She hadn't even told Vicki, though her friend had raised her eyebrows when Mallory had ordered a virgin margarita at their last get-together.

Logan had to be the first to know. And he would be. Very soon.

He was returning today after a weekend in Oregon. He'd met his son for the first time yesterday. He'd called Mallory last night so full of heartache and hope that she knew she couldn't keep the news to herself any longer. The timing might not be perfect, but it was right.

She was on her way to the airport now and she had it all planned. After she picked him up, she was going to take him back to her apartment where a candlelight dinner waited. She'd cheated on the meal, calling Luke to cater it. She wanted everything to be perfect, and her cooking skills were still iffy at best.

She spied Logan the moment he came through the gate at O'Hare. He looked tired but oddly energized. She greeted him with a hug. When she would have pulled away, he hugged her tighter and finished with a kiss that had her toes wanting to curl.

"I think you missed me."

"I did, indeed. And it got me thinking."

"Yeah? About what?"

"I'll tell you when we get to my place." He bobbed his brows.

"If you're not too tired from your flight, I thought we'd go to my apartment instead. I have dinner waiting and a little surprise."

"That's fine. I have a little surprise of my own," he said with an enigmatic wink.

The last thing Mallory expected Logan to do the moment they entered her apartment was pull a ring box from his pocket and drop to one knee. He'd said he had a little surprise for her. Talk about an understatement. The diamond winking back at her from the box appeared to be all of three carats.

"Wh-what are you doing?" she asked.

"You can't figure it out? You're usually pretty quick." He grinned.

"You…you want…"

"To marry you." He nodded and caught her in his arms when she sagged. They both wound up sitting on the floor. "I love you, Mallory. I want to spend my life with you. If you want to take your time answering, that's okay. I know things are a little crazy right now and they will be for a while yet. I can be patient."

"I don't need to take time. Yes! Yes, I'll marry you." She cupped his face, kissed him soundly and then sighed as he took over and lowered her onto the floor.

It was several moments before he helped her to her

feet. "Dinner smells good," he said. "Hey, didn't you say you had a little surprise for me, too?"

She nibbled her bottom lip, but then smiled. It was too early to feel the baby, but she swore she felt something wonderful flutter inside of her. "Yes, I do."

EPILOGUE

Three years later

"WE'RE having a baby?" Logan was smiling as he asked the question.

"The doctor says I'm due the first week in October." Mallory grinned in reply. "She could arrive on our third wedding anniversary."

"That would be quite a present." He put his arms around her and dropped a kiss on her lips. "And from your reference to the baby as a she, I see that you're hoping for a girl this time."

"I love the men in my life, but with you, Devon and little Patrick, there are too many of you. It would be nice to have another female in the house."

Devon had been coming to stay with Logan on alternating weekends and holidays since he and his mother moved back from Portland six months after the story of Logan's paternity first made headlines. The arrangement wasn't ideal. No child custody arrangement ever was. But they were making it work.

Of course, it had been rough on all of them in the beginning. Not surprisingly Devon had been angry, hurt and confused. He'd lashed out at everyone, with his father the prime target. Even when Logan had been devastated by his son's animosity and pain, he'd remained patient and, with Mallory's help, hopeful that eventually the boy would come around.

And he had.

It had taken Devon more than a year before he called Logan "Dad." Mallory thought it was apropos that the boy did so the same day Patrick uttered his first Da-Da. Things had gotten easier after that, and a real relationship had begun to form. None of the awkwardness that had accompanied their get-togethers during those first months was present now. She wouldn't say things were perfect, but they were close.

"What are you thinking?" Logan asked, pulling Mallory from her musings.

She meant it when she replied, "That I'm the luckiest woman in the world."

*Bestselling author Lynne Graham is back
with a fabulous new trilogy!*

PREGNANT BRIDES

Three ordinary girls—naive, but also honest and plucky...

*Three fabulously wealthy, impossibly handsome
and very ruthless men...*

*When opposites attract and passion leads to pregnancy...
it can only mean marriage!*

*Available next month from Harlequin Presents®:
the first installment*

DESERT PRINCE, BRIDE OF INNOCENCE

* * *

'THIS EVENING I'm flying to New York for two weeks,'
Jasim imparted with a casualness that made her heart sink
like a stone. 'That's why I had you brought here. I own this
apartment and you'll be comfortable here while I'm abroad.'

'I can afford my own accommodation although I may not
need it for long. I'll have another job by the time you
get back—'

Jasim released a slightly harsh laugh. 'There's no need for
you to look for another position. How would I ever see you?
Don't you understand what I'm offering you?'

Elinor stood very still. 'No, I must be incredibly thick
because I haven't quite worked out yet what you're offering
me....'

His charismatic smile slashed his lean dark visage.
'Naturally, I want to take care of you....'

HPEX0110A

'No, thanks.' Elinor forced a smile and mentally willed him not to demean her with some sordid proposition. 'The only man who will ever take *care* of me with my agreement will be my husband. I'm willing to wait for you to come back but I'm not willing to be kept by you. I'm a very independent woman and what I give, I give freely.'

Jasim frowned. 'You make it all sound so serious.'

'What happened between us last night left pure chaos in its wake. Right now, I don't know whether I'm on my head or my heels. I'll stay for a while because I have nowhere else to go in the short term. So maybe it's good that you'll be away for a while.'

Jasim pulled out his wallet to extract a card. 'My private number,' he told her, presenting her with it as though it was a precious gift, which indeed it was. Many women would have done just about anything to gain access to that direct hotline to him, but his staff guarded his privacy with scrupulous care.

Before he could close the wallet, his blood ran cold in his veins. How could he have made such a serious oversight? What if he had got her pregnant? He knew that an unplanned pregnancy would engulf his life like an avalanche, crush his freedom and suffocate him. He barely stilled a shudder at the threat of such an outcome and thought how ironic it was that what his older brother had longed and prayed for to secure the line to the throne should strike Jasim as an absolute disaster....

* * *

What will proud Prince Jasim do if Elinor is expecting his royal baby? Perhaps an arranged marriage is the only solution! But will Elinor agree? Find out in DESERT PRINCE, BRIDE OF INNOCENCE by Lynne Graham [#2884], available from Harlequin Presents® in January 2010.

Copyright © 2010 by Lynne Graham

HPEX0110B

ESCAPE AROUND the WORLD

Dream destinations, whirlwind weddings!

The Daredevil Tycoon

by

BARBARA McMAHON

A hot-air balloon race with Amalia Catalon's sexy daredevil boss, Rafael Sandoval, is only the beginning of her exciting Spanish adventure....

Available in January 2010 wherever books are sold.

www.eHarlequin.com

HR17632

HARLEQUIN® HISTORICAL:
Where love is timeless

**From chivalrous knights
to roguish rakes, look for the
variety Harlequin® Historical
has to offer every month.**

www.eHarlequin.com

HHBRANDINGBPA09

Stay up-to-date on all your romance-reading news with the brand-new Harlequin *Inside Romance*!

The Harlequin *Inside Romance* is a **FREE** quarterly newsletter highlighting our upcoming series releases and promotions!

Click on the *Inside Romance* link on the front page of www.eHarlequin.com or e-mail us at InsideRomance@Harlequin.ca to sign up to receive your FREE newsletter today!

You can also subscribe by writing to us at: HARLEQUIN BOOKS
Attention: Customer Service Department
P.O. Box 9057, Buffalo, NY 14269-9057

Please allow 4-6 weeks for delivery of the first issue by mail.

IRNBPAQ309

REQUEST YOUR FREE BOOKS!
2 FREE NOVELS PLUS 2
FREE GIFTS!

HARLEQUIN® *Romance*®

From the Heart, For the Heart

YES! Please send me 2 FREE Harlequin® Romance novels and my 2 FREE gifts (gifts are worth about $10). After receiving them, if I don't wish to receive any more books, I can return the shipping statement marked "cancel". If I don't cancel, I will receive 4 brand-new novels every month and be billed just $3.84 per book in the U.S. or $4.24 per book in Canada. That's a savings of at least 15% off the cover price! It's quite a bargain! Shipping and handling is just 50¢ per book.* I understand that accepting the 2 free books and gifts places me under no obligation to buy anything. I can always return a shipment and cancel at any time. Even if I never buy another book, the two free books and gifts are mine to keep forever.

114 HDN EYU3   314 HDN EYKG

Name _____ (PLEASE PRINT)

Address _____ Apt. #

City _____ State/Prov. _____ Zip/Postal Code

Signature (if under 18, a parent or guardian must sign)

Mail to the **Harlequin Reader Service:**
IN U.S.A.: P.O. Box 1867, Buffalo, NY 14240-1867
IN CANADA: P.O. Box 609, Fort Erie, Ontario L2A 5X3

Not valid to current subscribers of Harlequin Romance books.

**Are you a subscriber of Harlequin Romance books
and want to receive the larger-print edition?
Call 1-800-873-8635 today!**

* Terms and prices subject to change without notice. Prices do not include applicable taxes. Sales tax applicable in N.Y. Canadian residents will be charged applicable provincial taxes and GST. Offer not valid in Quebec. This offer is limited to one order per household. All orders subject to approval. Credit or debit balances in a customer's account(s) may be offset by any other outstanding balance owed by or to the customer. Please allow 4 to 6 weeks for delivery. Offer available while quantities last.

Your Privacy: Harlequin Books is committed to protecting your privacy. Our Privacy Policy is available online at www.eHarlequin.com or upon request from the Reader Service. From time to time we make our lists of customers available to reputable third parties who may have a product or service of interest to you. If you would prefer we not share your name and address, please check here. ☐

HR09R